My Life
is a
Soap Opera

A Novella

Kristina Stangl

Also by Kristina Stangl

The Enchanted Forest Saga:

The Curse of the Dark Horseman

The Sleeping Knight

The Emerald Prince

Silverheart:

Cupid's Serenade

Sex, Lies & Politics:

The Ambassador's Wife

Wake Up, Darling

My Life is a Soap Opera

Kill Me, Kiss Me

www.kristinastangl.com

DEDICATION

In dedication to my loving family. Thanks for always supporting my endless stories.

To my readers, thank you for following me on this ongoing journey.

To all the strong ladies and gentlemen out there in this world. Aim high and bow down to no one in your pursuit of happiness.

Lastly, in loving memory to the one and only, Jackson.

My Life is a Soap Opera

My Life is a Soap Opera

CONTENTS

My Life is a Soap Opera

CHAPTER 1

Election Night

"Just breathe, Katherine," my assistant, James Petruchio, tells me.

"It's not that bad," he attempts to console me, as he grabs a hold of my cold and sweaty palms.

"Really, it's not the end of the world," he says with a bright smile.

A smile that I wish could easily fade away and instead, be replaced with another form of darkness and bitterness that I currently feel brewing within my shattered heart.

"How can you continue to speak so positive about everything?" I ask him, while I simultaneously turn my head away from his gaze.

Currently, I'm sitting down on my green velvet chair, located inside of my home office, and trying my best not to have a nervous breakdown. As far as I'm concerned, my life might as well be over.

All of my dreams, ambitions and desires, it's all amounted to *nothing*. After spending the past ten years working in the world of politics, tonight, my career has finally come crashing down into the oblivion. My life as I've known it, is now officially *over...*

"So, you lost the election, big deal," James finally acknowledges the long-held truth, that I previously sought so hard to deny this past hour or so.

"It's not the end, but the beginning," he says with much passion and conviction. "You, Katherine Sharp, shall rise again."

"Really? And do what exactly?" I mock his optimistic kindness with the cruel pessimistic undertone of my voice.

"If I'm not the next Senator of California, then what was the point of it all?" I ask him, while also gazing directly into his hazel eyes. Eyes, that are as of right now, the only source of comfort that's holding my sanity together like glue.

"I might as well change my name and move to Alaska or better yet," I inform him, dramatically, "Relocate to a private island, floating out in the middle of the Aegean Sea. Because, if I'm not in politics anymore, then I'm no long Katherine Sharp!"

"Don't be foolish. Katherine, you are *not* married to the world of politics," he clicks his tongue, in disagreement. "The only reason that I'm still standing here in the shadows of politics, is because of *you*. If it wasn't for *your* strong will and determination, then I wouldn't have lasted all this time by your side."

And *that confession*, certainly, catches my attention. For the past three years, James has been my rock for everything. Without him, I'd simply be lost. He coordinates my meetings with donors, schedules my appointments with various doctors, sets aside time in my calendar to allow me to work out at the local gym and plus, he also plays the part of a dedicated chaperone to all of our public events as my sole partner in crime.

Overall, James knows my schedule *and* life better than I do. Katherine Sharp might be the face and star of the show, but James Petruchio is the brains and heart behind the operations.

Additionally, after going through a host of personal assistants—many of whom, I fail to remember their names or faces in the first place— James is the only person, who can successfully withstand my strong and diva-like personality. As an upcoming female politician, many insiders in the press have nicknamed me as the *Shrew*, with James, being the only one who can tame me.

But as offensive as that term might seem to outsiders, it actually doesn't bother me in the least. I'd happily be the *Shrew*, if that's what it takes to rise up to power. Bowing down to no man, as I fight my ticket to the top.

However, tonight, I officially lost the election and now, everything that I worked so hard for, really was all for nothing. Perhaps, even this powerful shrew wasn't strong and charming enough to win over the hearts of the voters.

"Don't worry, Katherine," James says, as he kneels down in front of me.

Looking at him, I can't help but express a weary smile. James Petruchio might be my assistant, but he's also lovely in appearance, too.

With rich and wavy auburn and copper-like hair, hazel eyes with a thick set of lashes, a soft and fair complexion and a tall and muscular figure, he's a stark contrast to my petite self with medium length and straight black hair, porcelain fair skin and violet eyes. Plus, not to mention, the age difference between us. He might be seven years younger than I, but he acts so much older.

Regardless, one day, I hope that he can find someone who's worthy of him. After putting up with my selfish antics over the years, he certainly deserves a good woman who can truly appreciate him. He might be my angel, but I'm fairly certain that I'm his devil.

"But, James, it's all over," I whisper softly, biting the lower edge of my lip, as tears stream down my flushed cheeks. "I lost the election so badly. No donor will ever reinvest in me again. My career is finished."

"Trust me, Katherine, politics is not everything," James confides in me, wiping my tears away with his handkerchief. "After all, my father was a politician, too. Remember? This job requires thick skin, which we both already know that you've got and then some. But at the same time, this world is also just based on sex, lies and politics. Don't get too lost in this superficial bubble. You're capable of so much more."

That's true, James' father was a former politician. In fact, back in the day, I even interned for him. Out of all my close associates, James grew up in the world of political intrigue. It's one of the primary reasons as to why I originally hired him in the first place. But now, that past history, has all come crashing down into nothing.

"You know," I begin to reflect aloud, "I spent most of my youth dreaming of this night. From studying political science religiously at my university's library into the late midnight hours to associating with the right crowds, and even my own appearance, has been meticulously tailored to portray the perfect image of a proper female politician. Dark pants suits, with no color. And I *love* color! Especially, pastels!"

"I know you do," he sighs, as he runs his hand through his thick auburn hair. "Tomorrow, I promise that we'll go shopping and buy you a whole new wardrobe with a collection dedicated solely to pastel clothing. Afterwards, you can burn your other attires. In fact, we'll even throw a bon fire in your honor."

Shockingly, for the first time tonight since the election results originally came in, I finally laugh. As it turns out, I'm delighted by the prospect of burning the clothes that represents my now soon-to-be past. Clothes that I once foolishly associated as articles of my identity.

"You can always try again, too," he points out, remaining my ever the optimistic sidekick.

"No, there's no point," I acknowledge this sad and bitter truth. "James, I lost badly. By a landslide. Only wining thirty-seven percent of the overall votes. At this point, the statistics can't justify the means of me running again. Plus, if I'm being honest, I feel burnt out, too. I'm thirty-five years old now. I think I'd like to do something else. But then again, who I am, if I'm not involved in politics?"

It's true, the name Katherine Sharp has become synonymous as being an elite member of the political world. The public, the press, my peers, and even, my opponents, will always recognize me as the *Shrew*. Plus, I've spent the past ten years working in this cutthroat industry.

From graduate school to interning at the capital, to running a successful nonprofit and eventually, gaining the senate nomination. But regardless of all of these accomplishments; in the end, I still lost, no matter how promising my political career had seemed. Heck, even the polls had previously projected my win, only but a mere week ago. How foolish I was to think otherwise!

"Come, let's get you to bed," he finally changes the subject. "You've got an early appointment scheduled for tomorrow morning."

"But what about the broken glass?" I ask him, shamefully.

Unfortunately, hearing the news of my loss, sent me into a daze. One way or another, the crystal glass of champagne that I was previously holding, managed to find itself thrown across the room, slamming against the wall and shattering into pieces. Like my career, this broken glass can never, ever be recovered. From celebration to devastation.

"Katherine, you can't cry over spilled milk. It's time to let it go," he reminds me. "I'll order you a new set this week."

With that faithful promise, I finally head off to bed. Letting go of all my troubles and stress. At least, temporarily, for now.

CHAPTER 2

Counseling for Fools

"Umm, is he also supposed to be here, too?" my fiancé, Luca Cambio, asks me sarcastically.

"Why not? He's my assistant, after all. Where I go, he follows. Isn't that right, James?" I ask my right-hand man in everything, directly.

Being the loyal and dedicated assistant that he is, James simply nods his head in agreement. One way or another, he always tries to make me look good in public. Even in front of my useless fiancé.

"Anyways, someone needs to take notes," I sneer. "It's not like either of us are actually paying any special attention to these ridiculous sessions."

"Notes? Really?" Luca scowls. "It's bad enough that James *lives* full-time at your penthouse. Even I don't have a bedroom at your luxurious home in downtown San Francisco!"

"Oh please," I roll my eyes, out of sheer annoyance. "As if you ever cared for a room! Besides, you've got that fancy mansion of yours in Marin! Plus, I don't recall *you* offering me a bedroom at your estate, either!"

"Listen, I'm not here to argue with you, *again*," Luca pinches the bridge of his nose. "After all, your father recommended that we attend these sessions together, before the wedding. So for his sake, let's just forget about this entire conversation."

"Are you certain about that?" I promptly turn to face him, as I point my index finger towards his chest in an accusatory manner. "Wasn't it *your father* who requested that we attend these therapy sessions, as an excuse to cover up our sham of an engagement? To remain on friendly terms with one another? After all, your father was only willing to invest in my campaign, if I agreed to marry you."

"Kathy…" he begins to mutter.

"It's *not* Kathy, it's *Katherine*, remember?" I correct him, as I stomp my feet angrily against the red carpet in the doctor's office with my stiletto heels. "At the very least, you should know your own fiancé's given name!"

"Fine, *Katherine*," he sighs. "We just need to make it until December, then we can officially breakup. Like we always planned. Apart from our fathers being best friends, you also needed my father's generous donation, while I needed to stay in his good graces to keep my status as the heir to his fortune."

"Well, that was *before* the election," I point out. "Now, that deal is moot."

"Wait, so what are you suggesting?" he stares at me with a surprised expression.

"Why don't we just breakup *now*," I gleamingly smile at him. "End things, before the doctor even arrives. What do you say?"

"Is that what you really want?" he asks me, with a hopeful look.

"Why not? You never loved me. And I never loved you," I point out this important key fact. "Besides, if we end things today, then by this afternoon, you can go back to being a playboy freely, without the added stress of having a fiancé looming behind your shoulders. Plus, if your father asks, then just say that I was too much of a shrew for you to deal with."

Luca, the typical blonde and blue-eyed European heartthrob, was a poor mismatched pairing with me from the very start. Him and I are like water and vinegar. We could never, ever mix.

"Just go back to being an Italian Stallion," I advise him. "I'm sure that your girlfriends are still happily waiting for your return, as we speak."

"Wait, so you knew?" he looks so appalled and offended by the mere fact alone, that I was already somehow privy to his infidelity.

"Of course, I knew," I sigh and rub my forehead. Already, I'm eager to put an end to this conversation, once and for all.

"Then, why didn't you say something earlier?" he asks me, nervously. "Did it not bother you?"

"Luca, I would actually have to *care*, in order for it to affect me," I admit. "So, no, I was not bothered. Your infidelity did not hurt me."

"That's a relief," he releases his breath and quickly resumes his dashing smile.

"Either way," I continue on, "Let's just end it. You can go back to being the philandering heartthrob, while I can reclaim my freedom."

"I'll admit, this prospect does sound tempting," he ponders deeply for a moment. "But are you sure that your father won't object to our decision?"

"Leave my father to me," I reassure him. "Besides, my father is vacationing overseas, right now. It won't be until weeks later, when he eventually learns the truth about our breakup."

"But your father is in close contact with mine. He wanted you to inherit the last name of Cambio. Are you sure that they won't conspire and force us to get back together?"

"I'll make sure that won't ever happen," I vow. "Worst-case scenario, I'll just marry another Italian in your place. Isn't that right, James?"

And for the first time since I've known him, I watch as my trusted assistant blushes in the bright shade of red.

***

"Where's your fiancé, Ms. Sharp?" the doctor asks, while noticing the empty seat to my left.

"There is no more fiancé," I tell him. "We've since broken up."

"That soon? Did all of this transpire, prior to my arrival to this appointment?" the doctor asks, most curiously.

"Indeed," is all that I state, with my chin held up high.

With that honest admission, the doctor quickly jots down some notes onto his notepad. Meanwhile, as I stare at him, I notice that our assigned marriage counselor is rather handsome. With dark black hair, bluish-green eyes and a caramel complexion, Dr. Hakim Khan is quite an appealing sight to behold.

"So, as you can see, doctor, we might as well wrap up this session," I continue on, "After all, now, I'm officially a single lady."

"Yes, I see," he says with a wild grin, as he writes down the last set of words onto his notes.

"In that case," he quickly drops his notepad aside. "Will you go out with me, instead?"

CHAPTER 3

A Night at the Opera

"Why did she leave Don Jose?" I ask Dr. Khan, as I lean against the balcony's railing. Luckily, for me, in honor of our first date, the doctor purchased one of the best box seats in the opera house.

After my last therapy session, Dr. Khan unexpectedly asked me out on a date. But was even more surprising than his question, was *my answer* on accepting his ridiculous proposal. In truth, I think I just felt caught up in the moment.

Under normal circumstances, never in a million years, would I have accepted his romantic proposal. The truth is that I actually denied his request two times in a row that afternoon in his office, before I eventually caved in on his third attempt. In the end, it was the prospect of watching the opera, *Carmen*, that finally won me over. Plus, losing the election has also forced me to step out of my comfort zone. Inspiring me to try new things. Exploring exciting adventures. I mean, technically, I am single now!

"To be with Escamillo, her new lover," he whispers into my ear.

Dressed in a slick black Armani suit, Dr. Hakim Khan is as dashing and as handsome as ever. It's a nice change from his more traditional white collared uniform that I've grown accustomed to.

As for myself, I'm finally back to color. Currently, I'm wearing a bold gold and sequin mermaid form fitting gown, which highlights my hourglass shape and showcases my decolletage. Meanwhile, my dark black hair has been swept away into a sleek ponytail that dangles from behind my back. Additionally, I'm wearing a shade of pastel lilac eyeshadow to match my violet eyes and accompanied with a heavy layer of black mascara on my lashes. Overall, it's a vast departure from my standard black pants suits, with natural and barely-there makeup.

Suddenly, I feel Dr. Khan's hand brush against mine. Seated to my right, he leaves his hand above mine and allows it to linger there for an extended moment.

Gazing into his bluish-green eyes, I utter, "Dr. Khan…"

"Please, call me Hakim," he insists.

"Ha—"

"Ahem," comes the voice to my far left.

Without bothering to turn my head aside, I instantly watch as a third hand comes crash-landing in between Hakim's and my hands, separating us like naughty school children. Treating us, as if we committed a grave sin. And before I know it, my hand is resting lonesome above my lap, while Hakim's hand returns back to his own side.

"Carmen might be with Escamillo right now, but Don Jose loved her *first*," James makes it a point to answer my previous question aloud.

I know, I know, it's crazy, but what can I say? Even when out on a date to the opera house, James still accompanied me as my chaperone. It's not my fault! Really! He insisted!

In fact, according to James, it was *his* sole condition on allowing me permission to date the doctor. So long as my trusted assistant accompanied us along the way, then he'd have no objections. A personal bodyguard to keep me in check, as James so eloquently put it.

In the end, I prefer a happy assistant than an unhappy one.

"It doesn't matter if Don Jose loved her first," Hakim sneers at James' remark. "The point is that she's *now* with Escamillo."

Already, I can sense the tension escalating, here on the balcony. Right now, I'm seated in the middle, with two gorgeous men to my sides. In a soap opera, this would be called a love triangle.

"Why don't we just enjoy the rest of the show?" I suggest, as I flip through the pages of the playbill.

Although I've never watched the play, *Carmen*, before; however, I do know that this opera ends tragically. From what I've read online, Don Jose obsesses over the title character, Carmen. To the point, where he actually loses his sanity and ends up killing her out of a fit of jealousy. Thus, proving that the moral of the story is that love, no matter the circumstances, can never, ever be ignored nor denied.

For the next few minutes, the men keep perfectly quiet and still, as we watch the remainder of the show. By now, we're past intermission and are viewing the second half of the performance.

"I'm truly enjoying your company," Hakim whispers into my ear, as he pops open a bottle of champagne.

Graciously, he passes two glasses down to myself and James, as he pours himself a drink as well. Afterwards, he places his glass down onto the table, as he reclines backwards against his seat.

"We should do this again soon, Katherine," he tells me with a beaming smile.

Without saying another word, I simply smile back at him. However, my smile is taken for granted, for at this precise moment, Hakim suddenly leans towards my side this time around. He might have tried to hold my hand the last time; but now, he's eager to kiss my cheek.

Glancing to my left, I watch as James clenches his fist, tightly. Is he angry? But why? He should be rooting for me. But instead, he isn't. If I didn't know any better, then I'd even go as so far as to presume that he might actually be *jealous…*

But just as Hakim's lips are about to descend upon my cheek, I suddenly witness a splash of liquid land across the doctor's face, missing me by mere inches.

"What in the devil!" he shouts out loud and immediately, he's received by a handful of shushes from the audience seated nearby.

"It appears that I lost my balance," James replies, nonchalant. "So sorry."

However, judging by his cold expression, I can tell that he doesn't look too apologetic, at all.

"You did that on purpose!" Hakim growls, angrily.

"Shush," I say this time, trying my best to defuse this tense situation. "Everyone is staring at us."

"So? That bastard destroyed my new Armani suit!" he roars.

"Bastard?" I'm shocked at the audacity of him uttering such a spiteful word. "How dare you call my assistant a bastard!"

"Katherine, please don't be troubled," James warns me, as he grabs a hold of my hand.

"Honestly, who brings another male escort to a date," Hakim huffs, in annoyance. "What exactly did you expect? A threesome or something?"

"Now, you've crossed the line," James quickly rises up from his seat, ready to punch my-so-called date.

But rather than allowing my beloved assistant from getting involved in this heated mess, I promptly step in front of him, instead.

"Listen," I begin, as I face my date-now-turned-into-foe, "No one speaks to me in that vulgar manner. And most importantly, no one, and I repeat, no one, calls *my assistant* a bastard!"

With the drink still in my hand, I throw the rest of my champagne across Hakim's face and pour the remaining droplets down his silk shirt.

"Come on, James," I order, with my chin held up high. "Let's go."

With our arms interlinked, we push through the red velvet curtains and depart the opera house early.

In the end, I don't care who Carmen chose. She can stay with Escamillo for all I care. All that matters to me is that I, Katherine Sharp, choose James.

CHAPTER 4

A Trip to Napa

"Ｊames, my hair is turning into a mess!" I shout aloud as the howling wind blows right through my ponytail, forcing the ends of my black hair to flip and bounce along with the breeze, smacking my behind in the process.

"Hold on," he tells me, as he raises the hood of our red convertible.

Currently, we are driving across the highway, making our way up to Napa Valley. Thus far, after losing the election, I've experienced two types of reactions about my loss from the general public.

Representing the majority of the population, the first reaction comes from folks who are blatantly seeking to avoid me as if I never existed in the first place, both personally and professionally. Strategically distancing themselves away from the disgraced shrew, who apparently, made a complete mockery of herself by losing so badly to her more charming and popular male opponent.

However, in contrast to the overwhelmingly dominant reaction held by the first clan, the second group of society represents a silent minority. To my own surprise, these folks are genuinely saddened on my behalf— many of whom, are complete strangers. As a result, several from this camp have been sending me condolence gifts in the forms of flowers, fruit baskets and cards. But the real truth is that they *pity me.*

Either way, I don't care for both reactions. In fact, I'd much rather prefer distance over pity. Katherine Sharp's pride does not handle pity all that well.

However, with that being said, some gifts have also proven to be rather useful. In the case of my good friend, Jennifer Yildiz, she invited me to stay at one of her world exclusive villas in the neighboring Napa Valley region, just a short distance car ride away from downtown San Francisco.

Years ago, I met Jennifer when she was still married to her first husband, John Barrett, the U.S. Ambassador. Back then, we used to mingle at various social events, luncheons and fundraisers, while she was still a prominent personality in the political arena. In truth, she was one of the few people, whom I genuinely liked and got along with.

Flash forward to a few years later, Jennifer ended up divorcing her husband, remarrying a hotel heir and reinvented her life, outside of politics. Now, she's happily married to her second husband, Selim Yildiz, is the mother to twin daughters, Rose and Daisy, and travels around the world in style, while residing in one of her husband's many properties found across the globe. And if anyone was able to successfully carve a new life for themselves outside of the world of politics, then it's Jennifer.

But then again, if my life is a soap opera, then Jennifer's life is a full out primetime drama. Apart from everything else that I mentioned, her twin sister also went on to marry her former husband, too. It should have been a fiasco; however, the family happily accepted each other's reversed pairings.

In the end, Jennifer's twin sister, Dr. Kate Stanley, became the second Mrs. Barrett and went on to have twin daughters of her own. Currently, Kate is still married to John, and has since transitioned her career over from an NYU history professor to an archeologist. Meanwhile, she continues to travel alongside with her husband, accompanying him as his partner to numerous international posts. And while he's busy dealing with the embassy's affairs, she's out excavating onsite to collect hidden treasures for various world-renowned museums and other private wealthy collectors.

And now, because of my political connections, I'll be staying at one of the most exclusive Napa villas as my weekend getaway. And to top it all off, I also have a wine tasting event scheduled at Jennifer's former husband's winery, Barrett & Son, too.

Ah, I can't complain. Fine wine and the great outdoors are the cures to everything deemed gloomy and dreary in this world. And if my good friend, Jennifer, can reinvent herself, then perhaps, I can, too.

***

"This view is absolutely breathtaking," James proclaims, as he takes a sip of his red wine.

"Indeed, it is," I can't help but agree, as I spread a generous serving of brie cheese over my saltine cracker.

Thus far, this afternoon has been peaceful and pleasant. After driving the past two hours on the road, we finally reached our destination. And today, Napa is as stunning as ever. Even in mid-November, the Northern Californian weather still resembles the summer season.

As a San Franciscan native, I've only visited Napa just a handful of times. However, whenever I do come up here to visit out of the blue, my spirit automatically improves for the better. In many ways, these vineyards reminds me a lot of Tuscany.

Secretly, I've always wanted to travel to Italy. However, given my busy work schedule over the years, I never previously had the chance to go and visit. But luckily, as a consolation, a brief road trip by car and already, I feel like I've been magically transported over to Europe. I suppose that for now, this trip will just have to suffice in lieu of the real deal.

But apart from my traveling dreams, Napa is a true local gem. From the town's rolling emerald green hills to the newly ripe red grapes sprouting across the valley, to the clear blue sky and bright golden sunshine, to the fresh air and cool breeze, for the first time since losing the election, my mind finally feels at great ease in my new surroundings. Plus, this wine tasting event couldn't have come at a better time, too.

After departing the city this morning, I skipped breakfast altogether. And while James is busy enjoying our latest bottle of Barrett & Son, I'm taking advantage of eating as many hors d'oeuvres as I possibly can. Luckily, for me, the winery tour was a short thirty-minute walk through of the company's factory and the rest of our time has been spent outdoors, seated on a wooden table with a marvelous view of the vineyard.

Although this tour only had less than a dozen or so tourists, I'm still trying my best to conceal my identity. With a pair of black cat-eyed sunglasses and a red satin headscarf to match my crimson A-line summer knee-high eyelet dress with golden lace trimmings, I'm hoping that no one around us will recognize me. Especially, so soon after the election.

"Are you enjoying yourself?" James asks me, as he reaches over to serve himself some fruit.

"As best as I can," I admit, as I grab a helpful handful of walnuts and add it to my growing plate.

"If you're hungry, then we can always leave and find a more formal restaurant," he suggests.

"No, that's alright," I reply, as a nibble away on a walnut. "Besides, I'm enjoying this lovely view."

"Ah, yes, it really is lovely," he beams, as he takes another sip of his wine.

"You know," James begins, "My family's origins are from Tuscany. In fact, some of my father's relatives owns vineyards out there in the city of Pisa, too."

"Your family still lives in Italy?" I ask, amazed that I miraculously gained a new connection to the region of my dreams.

"Yes, they still do," he grins at me, as he takes a bite of his strawberry. "Why? Did you not already know?"

"Actually, no. Your father never mentioned it to me before," I confess.

"Of course," James frowns. "It's all about business and no pleasure, when it comes to my father."

"Anyways," he attempts to redirect the conversation away from his father. A man, whom James clearly has little respect for.

"My family owns several vineyards over there," he continues on, "Maybe, one day in the near future, whenever you're visiting Italy, then you can stop by and pay them a visit."

"That's if I ever get a chance to travel abroad," I sigh. "I never had the time before."

"Well, *now* you do," he tells me, with a bright a smile.

A smile, that for the first time since knowing him, makes me feel a little shy. Why haven't I ever noticed how lovely his smile was before?

"I suppose that's true," I agree, as I reach over and pour myself a drink. "You know, years ago, I used to paint."

"I know," he winks at me, as he pours himself another drink to join me.

"What? How did you know?"

As my personal assistant, I expect James to know everything about my *professional* life. However, him knowing hidden parts of my *personal* life, greatly surprises and intrigues me.

"Call it research," James reveals, playfully.

"Ah, so you took the initiative to learn all about your boss, before working for the infamous shrew, after all?" I deduce.

"When it comes to *you*, I know just about everything," he admits, now, with a serious expression. "Even your deepest secrets and desires."

His admission is compelling. Just what exactly does James know? To tell the truth, he's still shrouded in mystery to me. For the past three years, I've only viewed James as my trusted personal assistant and nothing more.

Apart from our working relationship, I really don't know that much about him outside of the office, even though, technically, *we do live together*. But apparently, with all facts aside, that's *not* the same case for *him*.

"Okay, so tell me," I start to dig in, "Tell me, what else do you *think* you know about me, apart from what the press has already revealed?"

Reclining back into his seat, he crosses his legs and asks me with a raised brow, "Is that a challenge?"

"Yes," I reply with a single word.

"And if I tell you, then what will I get in return?" he dares me.

"Anything you want," I smile at him.

Honestly, this *is* James. What else could he possibly want from me, other than a bonus or a raise? Truly, I'm not worried. Not one bit.

"I'll tell you what," he says, "If I win, then you must grant my wish, whenever I call for it. It could be today, tomorrow or even, a year from now. Do you accept my terms to our challenge?"

Really, this is so childish. Just what exactly does he think he secretly knows about me? Either way, I'll humor him. Again, what more could a personal assistant want other than a raise or a bonus?

"Fine, I accept your terms," I concede. Using my deep and sultry voice, I purr, "Now, James, tell me my deepest secrets."

"First," he proceeds, as he takes a gloriously long sip of his wine.

Meanwhile, as I stare across at his handsome face, I accidentally notice just how lovely his auburn hair looks, when the bright sun shines down upon it. His copper-like hair simply glimmers, just like gold. Instantly, my heart unexpectedly begins to flutter. Why is this odd reaction happening to me, all of a sudden?

"Back when you ran your nonprofit, you used to instruct your former students on how to paint landscapes," he reveals with a proud smile, convinced that he's already won this challenge with one go.

"Yes, that's true," I agree with him. "*However*, any student who took one of my classes would have known about that."

"True, but are they also aware just how much you cherish landscapes? *Emerald rolling hills.* Similar to the hills also found in Tuscany, *your muse.* And the fact, that those same emerald rolling hills were also your most beloved scene to sketch during your classes? Your favorite teaching lesson taught above all else."

"Wait, how did you know about that?" I instantly stop drinking my wine.

This sort of information is way too detailed. Just how did James know about the significance of this scene? Or, that it was my former muse that I used to frequently sketch?

"Were you one of my past students or something?" I inquire, with much interest.

"No," he laughs. "I actually bought one of your portraits."

"Oh," I gasp.

Hearing about my former gallery feels like a reminder to a past life. A life that I once lived, prior to entering into politics. Before I started graduate school and interned at the mayor's office at the capital and eventually, working my way up to becoming a senate nominee, I used to run a nonprofit called Bianca & Minola.

After graduating from university with an undergraduate degree in art history, I decided to use the inheritance that I had recently acquired from my late grandmother's estate to manage an abandoned neighborhood gallery. Upon purchasing the property, I renamed the gallery after my parents and converted the back studio into an art school. A sacred place that was dedicated to teaching the youth in my local community.

For five straight years, I ran the gallery's operations during the mornings by myself, while dedicating my afternoons on instructing teenagers the basics of painting landscapes. With my paintbrush in hand, it was my first attempt on trying to make the world a better place, once brush stroke at a time.

In my view, having some acrylic oils and a few paintbrushes to spare was a far safer option than holding a weapon. And if I could convince more kids to take up the creative arts, then perhaps, they'd have a better future, too.

In fact, my gallery and studio were designed to be a safe haven for underprivileged kids to visit, free of charge. A place where they'd have the opportunity to receive professional art lessons, while also admiring local artisans from our community. A creative outlet to keep the youth busy and away from the world of crime.

But after five years of operations, I no longer had the budget to continue. By then, I had spent most of my grandmother's inheritance. Furthermore, I refused to seek any financial assistance from my grandfather or father, as well. In truth, I had too much pride to ask for either of their help.

And so, at that point in my life, I decided to shift gears and eventually, sold my gallery to an anonymous buyer. Afterwards, I enrolled in graduate school and pursued a degree in political science as my new major. And thus, joining the infamous world of politics.

"Okay, so my former career isn't so much of a secret, after all," I admit, as I gaze straight into his hazel eyes.

Eyes that are currently sparkling, just like gemstones. Why is James suddenly so attractive to me, right now?

"Alright, I'll go on," he replies with much determination, as he pours himself another glass of wine.

"You hate it when people shorten your name into a nickname," he says, with much confidence. "Yet, being called the *Shrew*, never bothers you. You'd rather be called by that derogative title than Kathy or Kate. Or even, Kitty."

"Oh dear, God, please don't call me Kitty," I slam my glass down, with droplets splashing across the table. "I've especially, *never* liked that nickname. I much prefer dogs, instead."

"So, am I right?" he asks, with a hopeful expression.

"Yes, it's true," I bite the lower half of my lip.

One way or another, he really does seem to know all about my most inner secrets, after all.

"The *Shrew* is more of a political persona than anything else," I explain. "I don't mind people calling me that, because Katherine Sharp in politics is more of a caricature who fights her way to the top. A rebel. And besides, I always loved Shakespeare."

"But why the opposition to a nickname?" he presses on.

"Because unlike my political persona, Katherine in real life is *me*. And I don't want to be shortened to anything less than my true name."

"I see," James grins, as he finishes his drink. "In that case, Katherine, the Great, may I proclaim my prize now?"

"Almost," I toy with him, as I wrap my arms around my chest. "You've spent far too much time in the company of Luca. Surely, based on our therapy sessions, you must have picked up as to just how much I despised him calling me Kathy. Thus far, observing that I dislike nicknames isn't such a deep and dark secret."

"Very well, I was saving this for last, so here it goes," he carries on, determined to win this challenge, once and for all. "Your favorite flower is the yellow rose. And not too many folks are aware about this fact, either. Well, except for *me*."

"Wait, how did you know that?" I gasp.

Honestly, this time around, I'm genuinely shocked. I've never revealed this fact to anyone else before. Not even to my closest confidents. This information really is my own personal little secret.

"Because it's the only flower that you didn't throw away," he happily laughs on.

"Everything else that Luca previously delivered to our office, ended up in the trash bin," he explains. "All except for the yellow roses. They were the only exception. You even plucked those flowers out of all your bouquets. Which, might I add, takes a lot of hard work and dedication, too."

"Okay, so you got me," At long last, I admit with defeat.

"So, does this mean that you'll grant my wish, after all?"

"Yes," I sigh. "So, what will it be? Another bonus? Or a raise?"

"Neither," he tells me with a straight face.

"Wait, what do you mean?"

"When I'm ready to reveal my wish, then I'll let you know," he speaks, so secretive. "But in the meantime, tell me something, why is it that you love the yellow rose so much, above all others?"

"Because, it reminds me of sunshine," I finally open up to him.

If he truly wants to learn about me, both inside and out, and not the persona of the *Shrew*, then I might as well start by being honest with him. Allow him to glimpse into my true world as Katherine, from my own two lips.

"In a world filled with sadness, trauma and regret, yellow has always symbolized a happy color for me," I attempt to explain. "To create the most exquisite landscapes, I'd always add an extra layer of yellow paint to my blues to get the perfect shade of emerald green for my rolling hills. One brush stroke of yellow and instantly, an entire portrait can transform for the better. But whether or not I'm an artist or a politician, it makes no difference now. Either way, in the end, my community still rejected me."

"It's their loss, not yours," he reassures me.

"It's okay, James," I tell him, as I wipe away a tear from the side of my eye. "I'm coming to accept it. I tried something and it didn't work out.

I'm going to be alright."

"And you will rise again," James smiles at me, as he reaches over and grabs a hold of my hand.

Under normal circumstances, I'd pull away from his touch. But right now, I don't mind it all so much. His touch brings me a newfound pleasure that I never knew was possible before, until now.

"And the rose, well, I just love roses. Especially, their sweet fragrances. Plus, it was also the favorite flower of my late mother, too. So, there, that's why the yellow rose is my favorite flower. Are you happy, now?"

Being the ever trustworthy and dedicated assistant, he promises me, "Yes, I'm happy now. And most importantly, your secret is safe with me."

For a long moment, I gaze into his warm hazel eyes. It's filled with comfort, reassurance and kindness. In the midst of my world swirling in disaster, from a lost career to a broken engagement, James is the only safe and constant factor in my life.

I might not know what tomorrow will bring, but at least I'm comforted by the fact that I'll still have James by my side, either way. The forever handsome and devoted sidekick, if ever there was one.

"You know," I phase out of my daze, as I pull my sunglasses off from my face. "Apart from your name and family, I don't know that much about you. You've been my rock for these past three years. However, I'm sorry to admit this, but I really don't know anything else. Are you even married? Do you have kids? A girlfriend?"

"No, I'm not married. No kids. No girlfriend. I'm just entirely dedicated to you," he grins, from ear-to-ear.

"But it isn't fair!" I cry. "You know so much about me, but I know nothing about you!"

"That's okay, you'll eventually come to learn," he squeezes my hand.

"Just give it some time."

With that heartfelt promise, I smile at his direction. It's a smile that captures the blissful mirth and thrill that I strangely feel brewing within my chest. I've never felt this way before. Being here with James, I'm truly happy. No longer am I saddened about my past failures. Instead, I'm starting to look forward to the future. Whatever that might be.

"Excuse me," a strange voice comes from my behind.

Instantly, I turn around and to my surprise, a see a man in his late sixties, dressed in a pair of black slacks and a brown leather bomber jacket, while also wearing a blue, red and white Dodgers baseball cap above his head. I don't recognize him, at all. However, he appears to be a part of our tour group.

"You're Katherine Sharp, aren't you?" he clicks his tongue.

"Yes, I am," I sigh. Honestly, I was hoping not to be recognized out here, today.

"Would you care for an autograph?" James asks on my behalf.

"No, no, that's okay," the man laughs on. "If you had won, then I'd ask for one. I don't want autographs from losers."

"That's enough," James angrily cuts straight to the chase. "There's no need to be rude. You can leave now."

"I didn't vote for you, just so you know," the man ignores James' request and selfishly continues on, "California needs a strong man in Washington, D.C., not another weakly female wannabe. A kitty with dull claws."

I might not know everything about James' personal life, but I do know one thing, with absolute certainty. If I don't find a way to resolve this crisis within the next few seconds or so, then James is going to punch the living daylights out of this guy and the press is guaranteed to have a field day with this one. I can already predict tomorrow's headlines: *The Shrew's Assistant Goes Rogue* or *Shame for the Shrew and Her Entourage.*

Either way, both stories are unflattering. Therefore, I must do something. Plus, he called me by the worst nickname ever: *Kitty.* Even Luca never attempted to call me that. Officially, the gloves are off!

"James, I'll handle this," I wink at my sidekick and squeeze his hand, as I rise up from my chair.

"Thank you for not voting for me," I tell my newfound foe. "Perhaps, I wasn't made out for Washington, D.C., after all, if it meant that I had to represent jerks like you."

"Excuse me?" the man is dumbfounded and appalled by my blunt and bold statement.

"Besides, sir, this is the Forty-Niner's territory, not the Los Angeles' Dodgers," I lecture him, with my chin held up high. "Unlike yourself, *this weakly female wannabe* wears red and gold to support our local team."

Suddenly, I hear James' chuckle and instantly, I feel much more relaxed and confident, once again.

"Come on, James," I smile at him, as I put my sunglasses back on. "This cat is ready to bounce. Let's go."

CHAPTER 5

Underneath the Stars

A few hours later, James and I are standing outside on the balcony and staring up at the stars. After fleeing the vineyard, we arrived to the villa and checked into our separate suites. Although my room is located right across from him, James' balcony has the best view.

Right now, it's seven o'clock in the evening, and we've just recently retired after eating our dinner downstairs at the hotel's main restaurant. But instead of heading directly off to bed, I decided to accompany him to his room to gaze at tonight's blanket of shining stars.

"Isn't the night sky so lovely?" James asks me, as he leans against the balcony's railing.

"Yes, it is," I sigh. "The bright stars… fresh air… it's utterly peaceful and serene."

"Do you see those cluster of stars, over there at the end?" he uses his index finger to point at the far right.

Squinting my eyes, I notice an outline of shimmering stars that appears to resemble some sort of a wild animal. From this angle, there seems to be a body and a head. But what it is precisely, I'm not entirely sure.

"An animal?" I ask him.

"It's a lion," he informs me. "The Leo. Your birth sign."

"Birth sign?" I repeat, in amazement. "As in, my horoscope?"

"Yup," he says. "A lion for a lioness."

"James, do you actually know my birthday?"

Honestly, I'm surprised that he even knew. Granted, he is my assistant. But still, we've never celebrated my birthday together before. In fact, I don't even recall telling him about my date of birth, either.

"August 15th," James proudly declares. "And I've always known, since the very beginning, too."

"Don't tell me, you're responsible for sending me those fancy boxes of Belgium dark chocolates on my special day?" I laugh on.

But for some odd reason, James isn't laughing. Is it possible that it's true?

"Wait, I always assumed that my father sent those boxes to me!" I cry. "Was I wrong? Was it really you? All this time?"

"Guilty as charged," James shrugs his shoulders. "I couldn't handle the thought of you not receiving a gift, even if it secretly came from me."

For a long moment, I just stare at him in awe. After my late mother's death, my birthday was a day that I sought hard to ignore. Because in truth, back when my mother was still alive, she was the only person in the entire world who appreciated and treated me on my special day. Plus, my own father neglected to remember the date. And after my mother passed on, I tried to forget about my special day, too.

Even Luca never cared to learn about my birthday. But now, hearing that I still have someone who actually cares about me apart from my late mother, is truly touching.

"Thank you," I whisper aloud, as I reach over to grab a hold of him.

"Of course," he smiles at me tenderly, as he tightens his grip on my hand.

"You really go above and beyond," I complement him, as I stare up into the night sky. "I'm a Leo and yet, I have no idea what your sign is."

"It's Libra," he replies, seeking to alleviate my restless curiosity.

Slowly, James moves to lift our arms high up into the air, as he points at the constellation located to our far left.

"I'm the balance to your feisty lion," he continues on, "You, Katherine, are destined to lead, while I'm meant to help you stay on track."

"But I'm not a leader," I confess, sadly. "I'm no one, really. If anything, I'm a failure."

"Not all battles are meant to be won," James tells me. "You lost your first battle. There will be more. Just learn from your mistakes and move on."

"But I lost the biggest battle of my life," I reflect. "Where do I go from here?"

"We'll find your way, *together*," he happily gazes at my direction and then, squeezes my hand.

Standing so close to him, I can practically hear his heartbeat. It's soft and steady. A stark contrast to my own, that's currently rapidly fluttering with each passing second. Right now, I feel like a jittery butterfly, ready to leap off from this balcony and soar straight up into the night sky.

"You really do know so much about me," I remind myself. "But again, I'm ashamed not to equally know about you, in return."

"Well, then, just ask away," he encourages me. "Ask and I shall answer."

He's daring me, that's for sure. And tonight, I feel a lot more courageous than ever before. After all, if I'm the lioness in this relationship, then I might as well take full advantage and get to know him better.

"Are you happy working with me?" I ask the million-dollar question.

"Yes, it's been a dream come true," he presents me with a beaming smile. "I'm happiest whenever I'm near your side."

Instantly, I blush by that honest and heartfelt response.

"When exactly is your birthday?" I attempt to inquire, with a straight face.

"October 9th," he replies.

"I see," I say. "And is there anything special that you want next year for your birthday?"

"Hmm… that's still too far away," James notes, as he runs his right hand through his thick auburn hair. Hair that I'm equally curious about running my own hands through, too.

"Instead of waiting for a future birthday present, why don't I collect my prize now for winning today's challenge?" he asks me, point blank.

"Your prize? Right now?" I ask, in surprise. "Do you want a bigger suite? After all, you did mention that you didn't care for another raise or a bonus. Plus, you're already my personal assistant, so I'm not sure that a promotion is even available beyond this role…"

"Kiss, me…" he confesses, with his face half hidden from behind the shadows.

"Kiss you?" I repeat, with my mouth opened wide in shock.

Really, this is so silly. A simple kiss on the cheek is a pointless gesture. However, if this is what he wants, then I'm willing to humor him.

Without waiting for his reply, I swiftly lean in and place a gentle kiss alongside his cheek. As I pull away, I notice the surprise look upon his face. Is he disappointed?

"That's not a kiss," he growls.

The next thing I know, he pulls me back towards his chest, and his mouth comes crashing down onto mine.

And his kiss is single-handedly, the best kiss that I've ever experienced in my entire life!

CHAPTER 6

Soap Bubbles

After James kissed me, I franticly fled his room and dashed back into mine. As unexpected as his kiss was, it was also equally magical, too. Just thinking about it again, makes me blush in the shade of bright red out of sheer embarrassment.

Recalling back to that memorable moment, his mouth tasted like a forbidden fruit. One kiss, and instantly, I was forced to surrender to his touch. With his plump lips and porcelain teeth intertwined with mine, sucking my wet tongue dry with an intense display of passion and desire, it was so easy to get lost in the moment. And for a long minute, I really did, too.

If I hadn't pulled myself and walked away from his embrace, then God only knows what would have transpired between us. Indeed, I might have actually foolishly given myself to him, both body and soul.

But if I had, then it wouldn't have been fair. After all, this is James that I'm taking about. *My trusted sidekick.* The only person in the entire world, whom I can blindly trust. The only one who constantly defends and protects me. The only soul who can tame my diva-like self. My equal. My match.

Now, with a few extra glasses of wine and a long luxurious bath, I'm determined to forget about that wonderous kiss. *I must.* For if I don't, then how can I possess the courage to face him again? How can we ever return back to being the same duo, as we were before taking this trip?

And so, this is why I'm currently lounging in my bathtub, soaking in a long and hot bubble bath, hoping to scrub away all of my troubles with a bar of rose scented soap. An excuse to hopefully, clean and float all of my worries away, just like the traveling rosy pink soap bubbles that currently surrounds me.

"I will overcome him, I shall!" I convince myself. "After all, James is younger than me. It wouldn't be right to be with him. Instead, he should be with a girl, who's much closer to his own age."

Scrub, scrub, scrub, I use my loofah to scrub off the extra layers of dirt that's clinging onto my naked skin. Attempting to cleanse my guilt of our last kiss, as if we committed a grave sin.

Before the election, my life was so much simpler. I purchased an exclusive penthouse, worked in a private office and maintained a firm set of goals. Each morning, I'd awake fully rested and ready to greet the day with a cup of black coffee and a rigid schedule. A routine lifestyle that would hopefully, one day include a seat at the senate's floor. Advocating for the policies that I believed in.

Granted, gaining my political nomination wasn't an easy task to achieve. Honestly, it took *years* of dedication and hard work. Plus, a phony engagement to a philandering heartthrob— but it's not like I ever planned on walking down the aisle with Luca. Love was never a topic of discussion for me. Instead, it was always about my career and before that, school. So, now, my current feelings for James are just so… so… *confusing.*

Since losing the election, my perfect bubble of a world is finally bursting out into the open. I am *not* a senator. I am *no* longer engaged.

Furthermore, in a month's time, there won't be an office or staff or even volunteers left in my building, for the campaign's funding will officially have run out. Plus, soon enough, I'm going to hear an earful from my father and Mr. Cambio about ending my engagement to Luca.

But none of these issues matters in the end, if I have James by my side. As long as he's still with me, then I can weather this storm. That's why I *can't* lose him. That's why I must *remain* professional around him. I don't want to scare him away, like everyone else in my past.

Since when did my life turn into a soap opera? I feel like I'm watching my crazy world unfold as a third person audience member in real-time, while on the set of a dramatic television show called *Love, After the Election.*

"Ah, just let it go, Katherine," I attempt to convince myself, as I take another sip of my wine. "It's not like you actually, *love him.*"

Putting my glass down onto the table, I close my eyes shut as I sink further into the tub, with an extra layer of pink bubbles covering my naked body. Love and James are topics for another evening. Right now, I just want to forget about him, along with everyone else in my life.

However, just as I'm about to enjoy this quiet moment of solitude, I suddenly hear footsteps coming from outside of my bathroom's door. Who could be wandering inside of my hotel suite at this late hour? I purposely left the *do not disturb* sign outside of my front door. If this is housekeeping, then I hope that they leave quickly.

But then again, what if it isn't housekeeping? Or even, an employee working at this villa? What if, it's an intruder? Apart from James, I don't have a personal bodyguard assigned to me. If this is a thief or worse, a stalker, then I need to be prepared to fight back and soon, too!

Rising up from the tub, I'm covered in bubbles from head-to-toe. But my untidy appearance is the least of my worries right now. Quickly, I grab a hold of my canary yellow towel and without rinsing, I swiftly wrap it around my naked body.

Searching for a nearby weapon, I instinctively grab a cordless hair dryer and grasp it tightly within the clutch of my hands. Creeping next to the bathroom door, I listen to the stranger's footsteps as they continue to walk against the hardwood floor of my bedroom.

Katherine Sharp might be a great many things, but I am by far, *fearless*. No one, and I mean, absolutely no one breaks into my bedroom unannounced! Especially, during my weekend getaway! Hell has no fury like the *Shrew* unhinged!

Without thinking any further, I instantly run out the door and confront my intruder. Clutching my hair dryer like a gun, I aim it directly at the stranger. Hopefully, underneath these dimmed hallway lights, they'll be fooled into believing that this is actually a weapon and decide to flee.

"Hold it right there!" I exclaim, as I continue to clutch the hair dryer tightly within my hands. "I'm not afraid to shoot!"

"Katherine," says the stranger, with a familiar male voice.

Alas, as my intruder steps forward into the bright lights shining from behind me, I instantly recognize that the thief is none other than my personal assistant, himself.

"James? What are you doing here? I almost attacked you!" I yell at him, angrily.

"With a hair dryer?" he asks in confusion, along with a raised brow.

"Yes!" I shout. "Or at the very least, I could have smacked it over your head! Besides, what are you doing here, inside of my bedroom?"

"Umm, you forgot your purse back in my room, when you fled earlier," he gulps, nervously. "I thought that maybe you needed it. Plus, I had a spare key to your room, too. Just in case of an emergency."

"Oh…"

Staring at James' deer-with-a-headlights-expression, I quickly realize that as of right now, at this very second, he's watching me with widened eyes in my current unkept state. With nothing else around my body, but a slimsy drenched towel. And because of my questionable attire, he's quietly standing there and looking entirely uncomfortable. To tell the truth, I feel uneasy, too. This entire situation is so inappropriate!

Dropping the hair dryer onto the floor, I swiftly address him and say, "James, I should go and—"

But before I finish my sentence, my towel accidentally slips off my body and lands straight down and onto the floor. And as the soap bubbles quickly dissipates from off my skin, I'm left standing in front of James, entirely naked.

And right now, to my absolute horror, he can see *everything*!

CHAPTER 7

Kiss Me, Kate

"**D**on't bother covering up," James demands, as he takes a step forward, moving towards my direction.

"But I'm naked!" I yell, as I close my eyes shut. Already, I'm filled with an avalanche of embarrassment and regret.

If I have to be naked in front of him, then I don't want to witness his expression. This entire fiasco is already horrifying as it is!

"Yes, I know," he tells me, with a hint of mischief lingering within his voice.

And this time around, I can practically feel his body standing next to mine, just mere inches away.

"Do you really wish for me to cover you back up?" he softly whispers into my ear, seductively. "I can always bend down and retrieve your towel. But is that really what you desire?"

"Of course, I do. James, it's the only right thing to do," I reply, with my eyes remaining shut. "Honestly, I shouldn't be standing naked. Especially, in front of you. It's not appropriate."

"Why not? We already kissed earlier tonight," he reminds me.

"I regret that," I lie.

"Well, I don't," he proudly proclaims.

His unexpected response certainly catches my attention and instantly, forces me to confront him. Without a second delay, I reopen my eyes and gaze straight into his.

"Did you really enjoy it? My kiss?" I hesitate to ask him.

"Yes," he gulps, nervously. "And if I'm truly being honest, then seeing you standing so vulnerable here like this, only makes me want *more*."

"More?" I ask in surprise.

"Yes," he confirms.

"How much more?" I press on.

Taking another step forward, this time, he pulls me towards him, forcing my mouth to lightly brush against his.

"Just kiss me," he begs. "Kiss me, Kate."

Perhaps, it's the alcohol still lingering inside of my body, but God help me, I want to grant his request. *Oh, so desperately.* If he wants to kiss me, then the hell with it. I'll give it to him! And if he wants to call me Kate along the way, then so be it! After all, James is the only exception to all my rules.

"Then, do it," I challenge him.

And *that challenge* changed the entire course of our relationship, as I knew it.

***

"**F**aster," I beg him, as he pounds merciless into my body.

Currently, we are lying down on the bed, with my legs spread wide and wrapped around his hips. A naked James is truly a glorious sight. Underneath all of his suits, I'd never guess that he'd be this firm. He has curvatures sculpted everywhere. Truly, he is a sexy hunk!

What begins as a kiss soon turns into a night of passion. Before I knew it, James carried me away and rested me against the mattress, as he moved to undress himself. A few minutes later, we are both left entirely naked, with our bodies pressed up against each other.

The next thing I know, he slips a condom on and enters into me with such brutal force, that I'm left feeling entirely breathless. Thrust after thrust, he ingrains his long, thick and hardened cock into my womb, as I scream his name, over and over again.

And as he pounds into my flesh with such savage desires, he focuses on licking and sucking on my nipples, as I claw my long nails against his bare back.

"Harder," I desperately plead, as he continues to pump inside of me, bringing me closer to the blissful stage of nirvana.

Sex with James is magnificent. Even on our first night of passion, it's like he already knows all of my soft spots and how to trigger them. Plus, this is James. Being so intimate with him… well… it really feels… *amazing*!

"Aaaahhhh…" I moan, as he spreads my legs further apart and continues to move inside of me.

And then, just as I think that it can't possibly get any better, he shifts our positions and places me right on top of him.

"Ride me," he commands, with a deep grin.

After the immense pleasure that he has just bestowed upon me, I'm in no position to deny him. Plus, I want to please him, too. Besides, I've never ridden anyone before. This is also a brand-new adventure for me. And so for James' sake, I'm willing to give it a try.

Sensing my hesitancy, he tells me, "Just rock back and forth. The rest will come naturally."

Following his direction, I do just that. Slowly, I roll my hips forward and back, as I sink further down onto him. At this point, his cock is buried so deep within me that it's almost like he's a part of me. That him and I have truly joined forces and have become one.

"That's it," he encourages me. "Now, try to pick up speed and move a little faster."

And so, I do. Rocking at a faster pace, I ride James, while my hands remain pinned against his shoulders. In return, his hands are tightly wrapped around my waist, holding me into place, as I move above him.

"Oh God, yes! Katherine!" he roars, as I begin to swing at an accelerated pace.

But just as I foolishly believe that this incredible sensation couldn't possibly get any better, he swiftly rolls me underneath him and flips me over. At this point, my ass is facing him directly, while my face is in front of the headboard.

"Katherine… my Katherine…" he utters, as he bends down and kisses my behind.

Already my heart flutters from excitement. Again, this is a new experience for me. Previously, I've never been this adventurous in sex before. But now, with James, everything is changing. And for the better, too.

A second later, I gasp as I feel his dick slide right inside from my behind. From this position, it feels so different. Much deeper than ever before. And at this angle, it honestly, feels so spectacular!

"Oh God!" I cry, as I bite down against the pillow.

And as I cry tears of joy, he begins to rapidly move within me. Thrust after thrust, he pounds into my swollen flesh, marking my skin with his fingers. Branding me as his own, over and over again.

Meanwhile, my womb is leaking with so much liquid that the sheets have become a complete mess by our union. But I'm not worried about that. Right now, all I care about is being with James. Having him inside of me and enjoying every last second of it.

And for the next several hours, I surrender my body over to my new lover.

CHAPTER 8

My Katherine

With the sun shining brightly against my face, I slowly open my eyes to greet in the morning. Right now, my head is pounding with a powerful migraine and my body feels so incredibly sore. As I toss in bed, I realize that I'm not wearing my nightgown. Or even, panties. Actually, I'm totally naked!

"What in the hell!" I mutter to myself.

I *never* sleep naked. *Ever.* I'm a pajama lover, through and through. So if I'm naked AND sore down below, then what the heck happened last night?

Suddenly, I hear heavy breathing coming from behind me. Slowly, I turn my neck around to see what's happening.

"James?" I cover my mouth in surprise. He's sleeping right beside me… and he's shirtless. Is he naked, too?

"Think, Katherine, think…" I whisper to myself.

Last night, I remembered gazing at the stars with James. We were laughing. Smiling at each other. Drinking lots of wine. A kiss. Afterwards, I frantically returned back into my room to take a bubble bath. And then, James came…

He kissed me, again! Passionately! With our wet tongues intertwined, saliva exchanged and more! But it didn't end with just one kiss. Instead, our kiss lingered on, as he touched me… *everywhere*. And I touched him, too!

Glancing at my naked body, I see evidence of his love marks on me, found all over my flesh. Especially, on my breasts. And then, suddenly, I remember it all. *We slept together. Multiple times. Over and over again.* It was the best sex of my entire life. His cock was so enormous, and his body was to die for. Now, just looking across the room, I see evidence of used condoms scattered everywhere. It truly was a wild night!

"I really did sleep with him!" I accidentally shout aloud.

My words certainly catch his attention, for he immediately turns to his side to face me. The blanket has fallen just an inch off from him— enough to show me a preview of his cock. If I wasn't in my right mind, then I would have gladly bent down and sucked his glorious dick in my mouth for breakfast… but instead, I can't. This is *James*, after all. *My assistant.* I can't treat him as my lover!

"James…"

"Shush," he says, as he grabs my hand and pulls me over to his chest. "Just go back to sleep."

"But James," I plead, nervously. "We… we… slept together…"

"Yes, I know," he grins. "And it was heaven."

***

An hour later, James and I are having breakfast in the kitchen. This exchange should be an awkward moment, but surprisingly, it isn't.

Like the professional that he is, James got up, showered and cooked us breakfast. A stack of pancakes with scrambled eggs. Out of the two of us, he truly is the stronger one. I haven't stopped blushing, ever since I awoke and got up from bed.

"Stop stressing and eat," he orders me.

Not wanting to argue, I quickly pick up my fork and take a bite of my pancakes.

"About last night," I start the long-awaited conversation. "I think we made a mistake."

"Hmm, are you so sure about that?" he confidently asks me, while he takes a sip of his black coffee. "Personally, I think not."

"James, you're seven years younger than me," I point out, thinking that our age gap alone is enough reason to explain why last night was a mistake.

"So?" he shrugs, nonchalant. "Age is only a number. Besides, I'm only regretful about one thing."

"And that is?"

"Calling you, Kate," he sighs. "I know how much you hate nicknames. I apologize."

"*That's* what you're sorry for?" I choke.

"Well, yes. Of course, I am."

"James, you can call me *anything*," I grant him permission. A first time ever to anyone, on my part.

"But most importantly, you're still in your twenties, while I'm in my thirties," I add on. "Wouldn't you rather be with someone who's much closer to your own age?"

"Nope," he wraps his arms around his chest.

"Why not?" I press on.

"Because no one else is you. *My Katherine*," he happily smiles from ear-to-ear.

"*My Katherine?*" I repeat, in surprise. "Since when have I ever been *yours?*"

"Since the first time I laid eyes on you, ten years ago," he admits slyly, as he reaches over to add another generous helping of eggs onto my plate.

"Now, eat," he demands, while carrying on as usual. As if his latest life-altering confession to me is nothing shy of being just plain normal. "After last night, you need all the energy that you can get."

"Wait, what do you mean by that? We've only known each other for the past three years. That's when I hired you, remember?"

"Actually, I'll admit, I haven't been that forthcoming," he proceeds to explain. "Ten years ago, you interned at my father's office in City Hall. Back when he was still the Mayor of Sacramento."

"Yes, that's true," I admit. "During graduate school, I did intern at your father's office at the capital. However, I don't remember meeting you there back then."

"You didn't, but I saw you," he tells me. "I was eighteen years old and it was the summer before I left for college. The first time I saw you, I thought I lost my mind. You were so incredibly beautiful and determined. Even then, you never let anyone push you around. You worked so relentlessly hard and maintained the patience to deal with my overbearing father. And God only knows that he isn't an easy man to deal with. But regardless, you were able to tame him."

"I still don't understand…"

"That summer, I secretly admired you from afar," he confesses. "I spent most of my days watching you from behind one of the cubicles. At first, I initially came to my father's office to prep for my upcoming college entrance exams. But then, once I saw you, you became my living muse. A reason to visit the office daily. I wanted you then, like I want you now."

"Why didn't you introduce yourself to me back then?"

"At the time, I didn't feel worthy of you," he sighs. "But after college, I decided that I was going to find you again, whatever means necessary."

"Is that why you applied to be my assistant?"

"Yes. It was an excuse to get close to you. Can you ever forgive me?"

"There's nothing to forgive," I smile at him, touched by his sweet and heartwarming story. "You've been so wonderful to me. I couldn't have asked for a better assistant."

"And now, lover," he winks at me.

"About that… are you sure that we should? I mean, I'm still older than you. I'm thirty-five and you're twenty-eight. There's still a seven-year age gap between us. Can we truly make this sort of a romantic relationship work?"

"Why not?" he gets up from his seat and walks over to my side. "Listen, I'm planning to visit my parents next week for the holidays. While I'm away, let's use this extended period apart, as an opportunity to serve as a breather. Take some time to think about what you really want out of life, Katherine. You don't always have to be the hero. Let your sidekick take the lead sometimes. I promise to treat you right."

Afterwards, he kneels down before me and kisses my hand,

while I blush in the bright shade of red.

"Katherine, I've always loved you," he whispers to me. "I can help guide you on your next stage of life. Please give me a chance."

CHAPTER 9

Me without James

Days later, I find myself alone in my penthouse and reeling from the aftermath associated with my wild night spent with James on our latest trip. God, I hope I never return back to Napa!

However, right now, he's gone. Three days ago, he left to board a flight headed to New York to spend the Thanksgiving break with his parents. And now, as a result, I'm spending this lonely holiday all by myself, as I reflect about my own impending future.

A few weeks ago, I was on full crisis mode, when I was forced to confront my disastrous crash-ending political career status after losing the election. Back then, I stupidly believed that devastating election results were the worst of my nightmares. But now, I'm not so affected by that loss, altogether. Instead, I'm more worried about my private life, including my relationship with James, moving forward.

Just what are we now, to each other? I simply can't ignore what happened between us that night back in Napa. I mean, *we slept together.* Drunk or not, it happened. And even though he wants to be with me, I'm still hesitant. After all, I was never looking for love. But lo and behold, it found me.

I suppose that my hesitancy for committing to a romantic relationship stems from my own upbringing. In truth, my parents didn't have such a great marriage. In the end, I guess that I'm secretly afraid that I will also end up like my late mother. A woman, who was destined to have her heart broken, over and over again.

But for now, I've decided to return back to painting as a form of therapy. And if I'm going to be alone on Thanksgiving, then I might as well use this free opportunity to finish a portrait that I started ten years ago. A painting that I attempted to finish, before I foolishly abandoned it to pursue a career in politics.

The portrait is ironically called *My Life is a Soap Opera*. I began this picture during my early youth, prior to closing down my gallery to attend graduate school. Back then, I used to love watching soap operas on daytime television. In between my teaching sessions, I used to paint for myself. And this was one of my last unfinished portraits that I left behind in my closet.

Perhaps, now, after all these past long years, it's time to finish this portrait, once and for all.

My Life is a Soap Opera is a family portrait on canvas that reflects my teenage life. There, standing in the center, is me. I'm wearing a violet woolen sweater, along with a pair of denim blue jeans, while my parents are resting at each of my sides.

On my left side, stands my late mother, Bianca Baptiste Sharp. She was the daughter of a wealthy businessman and socialite. My grandparents, Pierre and Paulette Baptiste, owned a French company called Foulard Baptiste, located outside of Paris, which produced and sold cashmere scarfs globally.

Even though my mother grew up in the United States, her parents lived primarily overseas. And so, to represent my mother's elite roots, on her side, I opted to paint my grandparents' Marin mansion, along with a colorful rose garden in bloom, with notes of tangerine, soft pink and crimson red roses.

Furthermore, to my right, stands my father, Minola Sharp. Unlike my mother, my father was not born into wealth. Instead, he married into it and thereby, eventually came to inherit the role of CEO to my grandfather's company upon his retirement. But unfortunately, for my late mother, my father did not marry her out of love—although, she originally believed it to be otherwise.

Sadly, my father was a cruel and unfaithful husband. With a string of unmemorable mistresses, hidden behind him. And in my portrait, I've painted several layers of dark shadows to represent these nameless women. The mysterious lovers of my father.

In truth, I didn't have the heart to paint real people near my father's side, since I felt like doing so would have been a betrayal to my late mother's memories. So at least by using dark shadows, I can convey the underlying message that my father is shrouded in mystery, which isn't such a farfetched scenario, either. Even now, my father has remarried and divorced at least two more times, since my mother's passing. Already, he's engaged to his-soon-to-be fourth wife.

Although I loved my parents dearly, growing up, our household was filled with endless drama. My father was always searching for love outside of our family's home, while my mother was constantly finding ways to capture her husband's wandering attention. Often times, throwing lavish balls and over-the-top social events to win his heart and love. And of course, I was always subjugated to their endless schemes.

In essence, this portrait represents my childhood. My parents. My past. A dramatic soap opera-like life, in which I was caught in the middle of. It's one of the reasons as to why I was so hesitant in the past to fall in love. I didn't want to end up like my parents. Stuck in a one-sided romance. Being part of a soap opera.

But either way, for better or for worse, this is the story of my past. And if I'm to have a future with the promise of a new beginning, then I must finish this portrait. At least, in honor of my late mother.

And the truth is, if my mother's dying wish hadn't been about me pursuing a career in politics, then I think I might have still been working at my former gallery to this very day. Even with my dwindling funds, I'm certain that I would have taken out a business loan to keep my gallery in operations.

After my mother died, that's when I decided to sell the gallery and change careers to hopefully, make her proud from beyond the grave. My late mother had a strong view of the world, and she believed that politics was the solution to end corruption. To offer peace to the masses. And to bring justice to the oppressed.

In reality, my mother had no control of her own personal life. She lived with the injustices inflicted upon my father. Every time he took an extended holiday away from her to run the corporation, she knew the hidden truth. It was never about business. Instead, it was always about another secret lover.

My father's philandering habits are probably the main reason as to why I'm not close to him. Apart from an occasional phone call here and there, I hardly see or hear from him. And in truth, it's probably for the best anyways.

But now, I've failed to achieve my late mother's dream. I didn't become the senator that she aspired me to become. However, perhaps, it's for the best. If my heart wasn't in it, then what was the point of it all?

Deep down inside, I actually do know what I aspire to achieve. I want my former career back. I long to pursue art again. I wish to reopen my old gallery. Restore Bianca & Minola back to its original glory. Teach my young students, once again. And most importantly, keep James by my side, at all costs.

Meanwhile, just as I'm about to pick up my paintbrush, I hear the doorbell ring. Answering the door, I'm greeted by a delivery person, handing me a sealed letter.

Curiously, I open the letter. To my surprise, I discover a wedding invitation. And just when I've convinced myself that I will never return back to that vineyard, I soon realize that the wedding is taking place in Napa. At the same exact villa.

One way or another, it seems that no matter how much I try, in the end, I simply cannot run away from my past.

CHAPTER 10

A Bouquet of Yellow Roses

"A toast for the new bride and groom!" the best man, Brent Summers, announces to the cheerful crowd.

Ironically, the best man is not only the groom's former stepbrother, but he's also the former husband of the bride, too. Another soap opera drama in the making!

As it turns out, Jennifer's cousin, Karly Summers, is the former wife of Brent Summers, a senator from Washington, D.C. Although I've never formally met Karly before; however, I am well aware that she's a famous and best-selling author. Not to mention, I've also read most of her romance novels to date, too.

About two years ago, Karly survived a hit-and-run accident, which left her with a bad case of amnesia. But that wasn't the end of her troubles. Apparently, her former husband had a secret mistress, Abigail Rose, who also just-so-happened to be his assistant, too. According to the headlines, Abigail was not only responsible for the accident, but she also later tried to murder Karly, soon after her hospital release.

However, during that same timeframe, Karly slowly started to regain her lost memories and, in the process, fell in love with her close confident and business attorney, Jake Valliant. Shortly thereafter, Karly divorced Brent and remarried Jake in a small and private wedding. They even honeymooned in the United Kingdom.

But according to Jennifer, their extended families were not thrilled about their decision to elope. Instead, they wanted them to hold a very public and lavish wedding. Therefore, giving into the pressures of their relatives— especially, on the groom's side— a second wedding was held in Napa Valley in their joint honors.

And so, this is how and why I ended up at their wedding. However, not being close to either the bride or groom, I find myself seated at table number twenty-four in the far back of the venue. But luckily, for me, thus far, I haven't been recognized and am currently seated next to two very entertaining senior ladies.

"Did you read Karly's new novel?" Virginia asks Beverly, the neighbor seated across from me.

Of course, they are discussing Karly's latest novel, *Loving the Duke*. Currently, it's a best seller and rated number one on all the charts. But what's even more special about this book is that many claim that the author actually based her lead characters, Jacob and Karoline, after herself and her new husband.

"Yes, I did," Beverly replies. "Do you really believe that the duke is based on her real-life husband?"

"I do," Virginia agrees. "After all, Jacob is too similar to the name Jake as it is."

"Indeed," Beverly goes on. "Plus, every author is known to pen stories based on their own real-life experiences. Don't you agree?"

And this time around, to my surprise, Beverly is staring at my direction. Was this question actually posed to me?

"Hmm… yes, I think I'd have to agree with you on that sentiment," I say. "After all, based on today's ceremony, the bride is clearly in love with her husband. I mean, why wouldn't she include their love story as an inspiration for her novel? It makes perfect sense to me."

"You know, I've always liked you, Katherine Sharp," Beverly happily smiles at me. "Just so you know, Virginia and I both voted for you. The senate could have used a strong-willed and passionate woman like yourself to shake things up for the better."

"Did you really, now?" I politely ask them, as I take a sip of my champagne.

"And if you ask me," Virginia chimes in, "You should marry that assistant of yours, before he gets away."

"Me? Marry James?" I choke.

Honestly, I didn't expect this suggestion at all. Since when did my love life become a topic for casual table discussion, in the first place?

"How do you know about James?" I ask them, cautiously.

Instantly, the pair happily burst into laughter.

"Darling," Beverly begins, with a beaming grin, "We've been following your love story from the very beginning. Why, we've read all the gossip papers concerning the two of you."

"You have? Are there really stories that have been published about us?" I inquire, with suspicion.

"Of course," Virginia replies, with a careless wave of her hand. "James Petruchio is the only man who can tame you. Or, at least, that's what all the gossip magazines claims to be."

"First of all, Petruchio defended you at your last press conference, amidst those nasty rumors circulating about your fiancé cheating on you with his yoga instructor," Beverly points out.

"And then," she continues on, "When your opponent tried to bash you publicly as the wicked witch, Petruchio wrote an extensive column in *The Examiner*, praising all of your creative talents. Why, if it wasn't for that article, then I'd never have known that you adored art. And if someone can love and appreciate fine art, then they can't be all that wicked, after all."

"He even jumped in front of you at the state fair to guard you, when a crazy spectator threw rotten tomatoes at your direction in Sacramento," Virginia reflects. "The poor man was drenched in tomato juice, from head-to-toe."

Come to think of it, they're right. James did do all of those things for me. From protecting me from that crazy spectator to writing a positive article about me in the press, James has been my rock through everything. He's consistently exceeded all of my expectations. Helping me in ways that no assistant has ever been obligated to do. And yet, he still did all of those things, just for me.

"But if you ask us," Beverly interjects, "A man who's willing to jump through all of those obstacles to protect a woman can only mean one thing."

"And that is?" I ask them, as my heart begins to race from the anticipation of their answer.

"Why he's in love," Beverly sighs. "My dear, that man is clearly in love with *you*."

"It's true," Virginia adds on. "The photographs can't deny the truth."

"Are there photographs, too?" I ask them with widened eyes.

"Yes. Do you really not read any of the papers published about you?" Beverly confronts me.

"Umm… actually no," I reply in shame.

"Well, you should," Virginia huffs in disapproval. "Because that man practically worships the ground that you walk on."

"And if you ask us," Beverly advises, "You should dump that Cambio boy and marry Petruchio."

"Wow, I had no idea…"

Honestly, right now, I feel like a fool. An ignorant fool who failed to recognize James' dedication and loyalty to me much sooner.

"So if Karly's life is based on *Loving the Duke*, then mine would be…"

"*The Taming of the Shrew*," Virginia and Beverly sighs simultaneously.

"Shakespeare's finest work in live action," Beverly tells me.

Just then, I hear a commotion taking place on the dance floor.

"It looks like the bouquet toss is about the start," Beverly comments.

"You should go," Virginia encourages me. "You might get lucky and catch it."

"I don't know…" I hesitate.

"Do it for your assistant, James," Beverly says. "Perhaps, this is the universe sending you a sign."

For some odd reason, I take their advice. Rising up from my seat, I walk over to the dance floor. Surrounded by a dozen or so other single ladies, I stand in the center, towards the far end.

And as my luck has it, I actually manage to catch the bouquet. But what's an even greater surprise is that these flowers are a bouquet of yellow roses. Perhaps, fate is sending me a sign, after all.

CHAPTER 11

My Life is a Soap Opera

It's now the first week of December, and James is scheduled to arrive soon. Meanwhile, I still haven't spoken to him, ever since he departed for New York. Although he suggested that we spend some time apart, the truth is that I miss him. So dearly, too.

Even with the seven-year age gap shared between us, I'm starting to believe that I can move beyond this issue. What once bothered me, no longer does. And the more that I reflect upon all of the wonderful things that he's done for me over the years, I'm inclined to give our romantic relationship a try. Especially, after listening to Virginia's and Beverly's advice at the wedding. Plus, if I'm following my own heart, I genuinely want to be with him, too.

Picking up my phone, I'm prepared to send James a text message with my answer. I don't want another day to roll on by, without telling him about my true feelings. However, just as I'm ready to grab my phone, I suddenly hear the doorbell ring.

Opening my front door, I'm greeted with the last person in the entire world, whom I wish to see: *my ex-fiancé.*

"What are you doing here, Luca?" I scowl. "We broke up, remember?"

But just as I'm about the slam the door shut in his face, his hand swiftly catches the door and stops it from closing.

"Just hear me out, please," he begs, out of frustration.

"Fine, I'm listening," I sigh, while tapping my left foot against the hardwood floor, impatiently waiting for his explanation.

"Aren't you going to invite me in first?" Luca questions me.

"Why? Do you need to be inside of my penthouse to explain yourself?"

"Please, I need some privacy," he pleads.

"Alright," I surrender. "Come on, in.

***

A few minutes later, Luca and I are seated in my kitchen and drinking a-much-needed afternoon cup of coffee. As a peace offering, he actually arrived at my door carrying a bouquet of fresh flowers. White lilies of the valley. Even after all of our time spent together, he still fails to recognize my favorite flower.

"I'll get straight down to the point," he says, as he takes a sip of his black expresso. "My father contacted me last night. Needless to say, he doesn't buy our breakup."

"What? Why?" I cry.

Honestly, his father's reaction is just plain annoying. What more must we do to convince Mr. Cambio?

"As it turns out, my father won't recognize our breakup with just mere words," Luca sighs.

"So, at this point, what do you propose we do?" I ask him.

"We need to do something more dramatic."

"Dramatic? As in a public breakup? Is that what you're suggesting?"

"Yes," he smirks, deviously. "You need to breakup with me in front of a large crowd, and it needs to be over the top. A breakup so ugly, that the entire world will be forced to recognize the dissolution of our engagement. That's the only way that my father will accept our fallout."

"Wait, so do you want me to slap your face or spit on you, or something?" I can't help but smile at that exciting prospect.

"Err… well… I suppose," he nervously runs his hand through his thick blonde hair.

"If we do this, then we'll need to attend a very public event together. A place where the press will be present all around," I brainstorm out loud to my new partner in crime.

"Well, this Saturday, I'll be participating at the horse races," he confides in me. "How about we breakup there, at the derby? You can accuse me of being the bad guy, while the press paints you out to be the saint. What do you say?"

"Do you really want to be portrayed as the villain in the press? Are you truly okay with that? Won't it damage your reputation?" I ask him cautiously, as I take a bite of my cinnamon green apple scone.

"If it means that I can return back to my old playboy life as a lone bachelor, then sure. I don't mind."

"You really are something else," I laugh. "Fine, for the sake of closure and severing ties, I'll do it."

"Great," Luca happily smiles with great relief. "Just so you know, Katherine, normally, I'd ask you to study on playing the part of a scorned girlfriend to perfection, but you already have enough experiences in politics to handle any unforeseen drama."

"Haha, very funny," I mutter underneath my breath, sarcastically.

Lifting my coffee mug up into the air, I make a toast.

"To our breakup," I cheer, as Luca joins forces with me and taps on my mug with his.

***

An hour later, Luca is finally gone. By now, I'm ready to draft my text message to James. But unfortunately, once again, I hear yet another ring coming from my doorbell. At this point, I really should dismantle it!

Opening the front door, once more, I'm greeted by yet another unwelcomed guest. Someone, whom I despise more than Luca.

"Hello, Dr. Khan," I greet my new visitor.

"It's Hakim. Remember?" he seeks to remind me.

"Yes, I remember," I reply, angrily. "I also *remember* you calling *my assistant* a *bastard,* too."

"I greatly apologize for that," he confesses. "That's why I'd like another chance. An opportunity to redeem myself in your eyes."

"There's no need," I kindly reject him. "Let's just let the past go. You can leave now."

"Wait," he stops the door from slamming shut in his face. "I brought you flowers."

Bringing his left hand over to his front chest from behind, he presents me with a bouquet of pink carnations and violet irises. It's a sweet gesture, but not necessary at all.

"Come to the art museum with me on Sunday," he pleads. "It's the opening exhibit to a close friend of mine. He's a local artist. And I need a date, too."

Hearing the words *museum* and *artist*, certainly captures my attention. If I'm serious about relaunching my art gallery, then I honestly should start mingling with new artists as well. As a curator, I'll need to network with various creative talents to convince them to lend me their art pieces to display as future collections. Hakim's proposal truly couldn't have come at a better time.

"One date, that's it," I tell him, with my arms wrapped around my chest.

"We can go to the museum, *as friends,*" I further emphasize.

"That's all I ask," he sighs, with much relief. "I'll swing by your penthouse around two o'clock in the afternoon. From there, I'll drive us to the venue, so we can attend the event together. But can I just ask for one special favor?"

"Yes?" I raise my brow.

"Can you not bring your assistant, this time? He kind of makes me nervous."

To be fair, I understand where Hakim is coming from. And so, to avoid another unnecessary altercation, I agree to the doctor's request.

***

Twenty minutes later, I'm back on my sofa. Finally, alone and at peace. With no other interruptions, I quickly grab my phone and begin drafting a message to James. And with a hopeful heart, I send my heartfelt confession over to my new lover.

Text Message to James:

James, I love you. Let's do it. But first, I need to go on two more dates with Luca and Hakim. ALONE. Please don't hate me. I do have a plan. Either way, just trust me. It's for our future.

Love,

Your Katherine

And if my life must be a soap opera, then so be it!

CHAPTER 12

The Breakup to Top Them All!

Come Saturday afternoon, I find myself seated on a bench at the stadium, right across from the horse tracks and waiting for Luca's race to start. Even during the first week of December, the weather is pleasant, sunny and cool.

Averaging in the mid sixties Fahrenheit, there are no winter jackets or snow boots in sight. Instead, most guests arrived to this venue wearing their finest derby attires. The gentlemen are dressed in proper suits and petticoats, while the ladies are showcasing their best formal gowns and sparkling jewelry.

However, apart from the participants and their horses, the real stars of this show are the ladies' hats. *All thousands of them.*

From silk cornflower blue ribboned bonnets to caramel weaved basket sunhats, to scarlet veiled pillboxes to baby pink mini hats, to violet wide brims to lime green fascinators, the crowd is inundated with a vast collection of derby hats throughout the entire arena.

But apart from the women, several men are also sporting hats of their own. Shiny black top hats to match their dark suits, accompanied by their respective partners who are enchanting flowers to their sides. Overall, it's a lovely scene that appears as if it's been plucked straight out of a romantic fairy tale.

Meanwhile, I also arrived to this event dressed in my very best. Currently, I'm wearing a white lace below the knee fitted dress, which covers my arms and chest. There are also black and white striped ribbons that are attached to the right side of my chest and connecting downwards along my waist.

Furthermore, I'm also sporting a wide brimmed sized matching hat and a pair of pearl earrings. What can I say? My inspiration for today's outfit comes straight from the character of Eliza Doolittle from the classic film, *My Fair Lady*. In hindsight, I figured that if I must attend a derby, then I might as well come dressed as my favorite fictional character.

Meanwhile, the stadium is filled with a large crowd and most importantly, reporters and their camera crews. So, if Luca and I are truly tasked on putting on a grand show in front of all these folks, then our breakup will surely be accepted. It must!

Unfortunately, the sad truth is that we don't exactly have a solid plan. Or at the very least, *I* don't have an actual plan. The fact is, I'm improvising here. One way or another, I just need to draw enough attention and do something so incredibly outrageous and over the top. Force the world to believe that Luca and I are truly finished, once and for all.

As far as the public is concerned, him and I are *still* engaged. After all, neither of us have formally announced to the world that our relationship is over. Thus far, our families are the only individuals who are privy to our separation. But even then, apparently, our parents— including my own father— failed to recognize the dissolution of our engagement. And so, now, I'm forced to go to the extremes. If I want a future with James, then first, I must formally end my engagement to

Luca!

But how should I end this sham of a union? Should I go all out shrew, and throw a shoe at him on the horse tracks? Or perhaps, accuse him of fraud and rigging the race in his favor to win?

No, I couldn't possibly do that. It would be too harsh and unfair. Even though I desperately desire to breakup with Luca; however, I also don't want to completely destroy his reputation in the process. Especially, in front of the eyes of his beloved country club.

"Doesn't Luca look so dreamy today?" I hear a young female voice speak from behind me.

"Yes, he's gorgeous," sighs another female.

Staring straight across, I instantly spot Luca, along with his white stallion, Biscuit. Resembling the famous star that he is, Luca proudly struts the arena, while dressed in his finest sporting attire. With brown leather boots, khaki slacks, a white collared blouse, a hunter green satin vest, and his dirty blonde hair slicked back, he looks just like a male model plucked straight out of a runway.

Honestly, I understand why he's a playboy. After all, most women around us used to always fuss about him… except for *me*. Even with his dashing good looks and charming personality, it was still never enough to win me over. Maybe, because at the end of the day, he just wasn't James. Perhaps, I've always secretly loved my assistant from the very beginning, after all.

"I wish he were my fiancé," a third female huffs.

"If only it could be…" daydreams a fourth.

Turning around, I spot the group of ladies fawning over Luca. Based on my brief observation, they all appear to be in their early twenties.

Discreetly, I count them. All ten of them. If I didn't know any better, then I'd say that they must be his fan girls. A club completely devoted to worshiping my soon-to-be-ex-fiancé. And suddenly, at long last, I finally have a grand idea!

"Do you ladies really admire Luca Cambio?" I pose my question to these group of adoring females.

"Of course!" exclaims the girl in the middle. "We've been following him, ever since he started modeling five years ago. Adele, here wants to marry him!"

"Excuse me," interrupts another. "I also want to marry him, too!"

"If only we could get his autograph or picture or something," sighs another.

Perhaps, I can kill two birds with one stone, after all. Make both these girls AND my dreams come true. All at the very same time.

"I actually know him," I happily smile at them.

Instantly, all ten women revert their attentions at me.

"Can you really help us to get his autograph?"

"His autograph?" I sneer at such a suggestion. "I can do even *better*."

"Better???" all ten replies in awe.

"I can get each of you a date with him," I grin. "But first, I'm going to need your help."

Needless to say, I gained ten new allies that very afternoon.

***

With a bronze trophy resting in his hand, I slap Luca's face and *hard*, with the cameras rolling right in front of us, capturing every last detail.

"How dare you cheat on me with Adele?" I yell at him, as his face turns bright red from the impact caused by my most recent smack.

"I'm sorry?" Luca utters, uncertain on how to properly respond to this very public altercation.

"Not to mention, you broke Grace's, Rebecca's, Mina's, Natalie's and Joyce's hearts, too!" I add.

"Umm… I did?" his eyes widened, surprised by the fact that I somehow managed to bring an entire harem of unfamiliar young females to stand behind me, as they serve as real-life actors in this soap opera-like drama that's currently unfolding in real-time, right before our very eyes.

"Yes, you did," I tell him, with my hands resting alongside my hips. "And not only did you break their hearts, but you also broke Helena's heart, too! Especially, when you stole her away from her boyfriend!"

"I did?" he scratches his head.

"Yes, and Anastasia's heart, too!"

"How?"

"When you abandoned her at the hospital! You were with *me*, while she was fighting for her life after the surgery!"

"Oh my! How cruel!" I hear the audience gasp and click their tongues at our very loud and most importantly, *public* conversation.

"But that's not the worst!" I continue on, now facing the crowd of onlookers.

"You ruined Laura's and Beth's lives the most!"

"I did? How?"

"Don't you know?" I stare at him with my brow raised.

For all of Luca's worth, he's doing great. Taking my wrath of a scorned fiancé without any complaints. I guess my years in politics made me a great actress, after all.

"They're pregnant!" I shout as loud as I possibly can, so that the entire world can hear. "And in case you're wondering, you're the father! Congratulations on having five children!"

"Five children?" Luca nervously gulps. "But how… is… that possible?"

"Simple," I smile on, "Laura is expecting twins… while Beth is pregnant with triplets. Hence, *five children.*"

"Shameful!" I hear a lady in the audience exclaim, as she then, proceeds to faint onto the ground.

Determined to end this charade once and for all, I conclude my act by saying, "And due to these unforgiveable reasons, I can no longer marry you in good faith, Luca Cambio. Our engagement is officially over!"

And to my sheer surprise, I'm greeted with a handful of cheers and claps from the crowd, along with a standing ovation. It seems that our act finally won them over. As far as the press is concerned, Luca and I are now history.

As a parting farewell, I walk over to Luca's side and lean against his ear.

"You owe each one of these girls a proper date," I whisper, as I pat his back.

Sighing underneath his breath, Luca simply says, "Thank you."

And for the man who loves women, I just gifted him a total of ten. A fine parting gift to my former fiancé, I must say.

CHAPTER 13

An Afternoon at the Museum

"Are you enjoying this collection?" the doctor asks me, anxiously waiting for my honest feedback.

Indeed, his friend, Martin von Helmsberg, is a highly talented artist. His unique style is exquisite. With a focus on still life, the portraits that I've observed thus far are depictions of various fruits. Primarily tropical fruits, such as bananas, pineapples, mangos and kiwis. Although von Helmsberg's portraits are decent, it's his other works of art that have truly captured my attention. In particular, his sculptures.

"His portraits are lovely," I reply. "But to be perfectly honest, I actually enjoyed his collection of sculptures even more."

"Really?" Hakim asks, in surprise. "I thought you'd relish on his portraits best of all. Personally, I find them to be more practical for use. In fact, my own apartment could use a few still life pieces on my kitchen's wall, rather than a bulky statue."

"Granted, I understand your view, too," I say to the doctor. "As for myself, I appreciate the specialized technique that von Helmsberg engages in to carve the vivid facial expressions onto his statues. It's almost as if they're real people, captured in stone. In my opinion, I find him to be very talented, indeed."

"So, do you approve of my friend's artwork?" he asks me directly.

"Yes, I do," I nod. "And in the future, I'd also like to collaborate with him, too."

"Interesting," Hakim notes. "Do you plan to take up art as a new hobby?"

"Not as a hobby, but as a new career," I confess. "I'm thinking about opening an art gallery of my own. Returning back to my old profession, before I got into politics."

"Does this mean that you're officially done with politics, altogether?"

"Indeed, I am," I happily sigh. "At this point, I'm ready for a new beginning."

With an approving smile, Hakim says, "You know, Katherine Sharp, you are an inspiration. Proof that there's still a life worth living at the end of the storm."

"I am?" His words certainly catch me by surprise.

"Yes, you are," he nods his head. "And the truth is, I understand you, too."

"How so?" I inquire.

"Well, about two years ago, I used to work at the General Hospital in Washington, D.C., in the emergency department," he explains. "Back then, I specialized on treating patients recovering from head trauma. In fact, Karly Summers, the famous romance author, was one of my patients."

"Really? Karly Summers?" I repeat in amazement. "I just recently attended her wedding, too."

"Yes, the very same one," he grins. "And after her case, I decided to leave the hospital, and move out to the west coast to open my own practice. With my joint degrees in biology and psychology, this time around, I wanted to focus on therapy. And I have no regrets. My life is certainly more peaceful than it was when I previously worked at the hospital. Overall, it was too hectic and stressful in that environment."

"So, what you're saying is that you also changed career paths, too?"

"Yes. And so, I believe that I can relate to where you're coming from," he sympathizes with me.

"I see," I say, as I stare into his bluish-green eyes. "Thank you for sharing your story."

Taking a step forward towards my direction, he says, "I still have one last confession."

"And that is?"

"The truth is that I originally asked you out on a date, because I wanted to test out a theory of mine," he reveals, with much embarrassment.

"What?" I choke.

Hearing that I was someone's experiment doesn't make me feel too happy. Not one bit.

"I wanted to see if I could meet someone who could capture my heart. And as beautiful and as wonderful as you are, I don't think that we turned out to be such a great match for each other, after all," he nervously admits, as he brushes a loose strand of my black hair dangling over my face and gently tucks it behind my ear.

"You don't need to tell me, I already know," I gaze directly at him, with my violet eyes. "Besides, technically, I'm with someone else. In fact, as I speak, he's well aware that I'm currently touring the museum with you. *As a friend.*"

"And that would be your assistant, right? James?" he chuckles.

"Yes, it's James," I announce, proudly.

"Good for you, Katherine. At least one of us, can still be happy."

"But what about you? Why did you feel the urge to use me as a test subject in your personal experiment?"

Taking a step back, Hakim runs his hand through his thick set of black hair and releases a deep sigh. Whatever it is that he wants to reveal to me, it's not something that he's too proud or happy to speak about out loud.

"I'm engaged," he admits with great frustration.

"You're engaged? Then why did you—"

"She's an acquaintance of mine from Pakistan," Hakim interjects. "We've never met each other before face-to-face, but our parents are good friends. It's already been decided by our extended families to marry. Come next spring, I'll become a husband to a total stranger. That's why I asked you out on a date, sporadically. I wanted to experiment on how it would feel like to date a stranger. In my mind, I foolishly believed that if I could easily fall in love with you, then I could also easily fall in love with her, too, But I guess in the end, love isn't so easy to achieve. No matter the intention."

"Ah, that makes perfect sense," I deduce.

In most circumstances, I realize that plenty of women would be terribly appalled by such an odd confession; however, in my case, I'm not. Rather, I'm actually relieved. Because if the doctor isn't interested in me romantically, then it means that we can truly remain as friends. And at this stage in my life, I prefer more allies than enemies.

"Can you forgive me?" he pleads.

"Of course," I smile at him.

"But," I add on, "If you're truly sorry and genuinely want to make it up to me, then please give me the business card to Martin von Helmsberg. I could use his talents in the future."

"Done," Hakim vows.

Happily, I'm thrilled. Already, I might have just locked in with a solid business deal with my first new collaborator.

"But what about you?" I ask this time, out of concern. "Are you okay marrying someone, whom you haven't yet met?"

"Well, I'm planning to travel to Pakistan next month," Hakim explains. "I'll meet her then. But for now, I make no promises."

"What's her name?"

"Saliha," he tells me.

"That's a lovely name. Perhaps, you might come to like her, after all?"

"Perhaps, or perhaps not," he replies sternly. "But either way, a lovely name or face is no more than a pretty statue. It's the heart that matters above all else."

"Truer words have never been spoken," I agree wholeheartedly with his sentiments.

Wanting to end this date on a positive note, I reach over and extend my hand over to him.

"Shall we start a new chapter in our friendship?" I ask him, with a shy smile.

"Come over here," he says and before I know it, he gives me a bear hug and kisses the top of my forehead.

And just as I pull away from his embrace, I see a light flash before my eyes. One way or another, a photographer has just snapped a picture of us and is currently, running down the hallway and about to exit out of the museum.

CHAPTER 14

The Scandalous Shrew

"The Scandalous Shrew," I read out loud, as I sip my morning coffee at the breakfast table. "You'd think by now, they'd come up with a much better headline."

Glancing at my phone this morning, I manage to come across the latest press release about yours truly. It reads as the following:

The Scandalous Shrew

After the devastating breakup of Katherine Sharp and her former model and billionaire heir fiancé, Luca Cambio, it seems that the disgraced heartthrob wasn't the only person who was unfaithful in their union. While the crowd cheered on in support of Ms. Sharp for standing up to her philandering ex-partner— who is also rumored to have at least ten known lovers, with two of them pregnant with either twins or triplets at the very same time! — at the derby, as it turns out, Ms. Sharp might not be so innocent either, after all.

According to various reliable sources, Ms. Sharp was also seen in the company of a handsome doctor this past weekend. Rumor has it, that this doctor already has a fiancé in a foreign land, and has been dating Ms. Sharp for quite a while. Just recently, they were also seen visiting the opera house together, along with a second man by her side. At this rate, Ms. Sharp might have a few secret lovers of her own.

It's a good thing that Ms. Sharp lost the election. Otherwise, we'd have another scandal brewing in Washington, D.C., yet again!

"There's no way of avoiding them," I sigh. "In their eyes, I will forever be the *Shrew*."

"We can always change that negative narrative," James suggests, as he places a stack of freshly cooked pancakes in front of me, along with a second cup of hot coffee.

"Yeah? And how so?" I ask him, with much skepticism.

"Give them something new to talk about," he casually replies, as he pulls me over to his side.

By now, James is back in town and as of yesterday, we're officially dating. And since James already has a room in my penthouse, he didn't even need to bother to move in. Everything just transitioned easily for us as a new couple.

"What else is there to talk about?" I lean against his warm chest. "My reputation is sealed. According to these reports, I'm forever the villain."

"Then, I'll give you a new name," he suggests.

"What do you mean?" I lift my head up to stare at his face.

"Perhaps, Katherine Sharp has been the villain for far too long," he reflects. "How about we change your name to Katherine Petruchio?"

"Petruchio? But that's your name? Why should I ever—"

Suddenly, to my heart stopping surprise, he proceeds to bend down on one knee. And for the first time in my entire life, I'm truly left speechless.

"Katherine Sharp, will you marry me?"

CHAPTER 15

The Taming of the Shrew

"You can't possibly want to marry me!" I scream, as I flee to a far corner of the room.

Chasing me down, James pins me against the wall. And right now, I'm trapped in between his two arms.

"And why not?" he speaks as calm as ever, with his brows raised up high.

"Because… because…" I stutter.

"Because…" he repeats after me.

"Because we just got together and…"

"And…"

"I'm afraid that I'll eventually scare you away," I close my eyes shut, as I confess my true fears to him. "After all, I'm the *Shrew*. And even though you might be able to tame me now, but will that always be the same case in the future, too?"

"Katherine, please open your eyes and look at me."

"No, I can't…"

"Yes, you can. And you will," he demands, as he places his hands against my face so effortlessly.

Slowly, I open my eyes to meet his. His hazel eyes are warm and comforting. Instantly, my fears are erased from my mind.

"Listen to me, carefully," he begins, "I might have used that silly article as an excuse for us to marry; but the truth is that I'm madly in love with you. Katherine, *I've always loved you*. And now that we're finally together, I want to use this opportunity to claim you as my wife and show you off to the entire world that you're mine."

"You do?" I ask with widened eyes.

"Yes," he sighs. "And for the record, you don't need any taming. It's never been about that. Instead, it's about me *complementing you*."

"Complementing me?" I echo.

"Katherine, you never needed taming," he continues on, "We complement each other. We belong to each other. *Just you and me*."

"We do?" I ask in surprise.

"Yes," he joyfully grins, from ear-to-ear. "You, Katherine, bring out the best in me. You make me work harder to become the best. I want to be a man that's worthy of your affection. Each day, you bring me joy. I admire your eagerness, determination, strong work ethics, and your kick-ass personality. You're my girl, and I will always be your number one fan."

"James, that's so incredibly sweet," I admit, as tears begin to stream down my cheeks.

"Katherine, I love you," James confesses. "And I wouldn't want to change not a single thing about you. Not even, a loose strand of your lovely dark hair. In fact, if you want, you can keep your maiden name.

But preferably, I'd rather have you take my surname, as a symbol of my love and devotion to you."

"Oh James," I sniff my nose, as I wipe away my tears. "I love you, too. And yes, we can give it a try."

"So, does this mean that you'll marry me?" he eagerly asks, as he wraps his arms around my waist.

"Yes, of course I will," I smile back at him. "And I'll take your surname, too."

"Katherine Petruchio. It does have a nice ring to it," he proudly beams, as he leans forward and places a soft kiss alongside my lips.

In the end, Katherine Sharp might be my birthname, but in recent years, that version of my name has also inadvertently evolved to become a villainous caricature in modern-day American politics. But perhaps, as Katherine Petruchio, I can shed my past and experience a fresh start with a brand-new identity, moving forward.

Besides, with a fresh bouquet of yellow roses resting above my kitchen table, I realize that James is the only person who gets me. And for that, I am truly grateful to have met him and to have him as my mate.

CHAPTER 16

Happily Ever After

With an amethyst princess-cut diamond engagement ring to match my eyes and securely placed around my finger, I brush my last coat of paint onto a portrait that I started ten years. At long last, *My Life is a Soap Opera*, is now complete. And in honor of the reopening of my former art gallery, I plan to include this unique piece of art as part of an upcoming future collection.

After my recent engagement, I came to learn a few more secrets about my new fiancé. For one, it turns out that James was the anonymous buyer who previously purchased my old art gallery. And not only did he purchase the gallery, but he also never rented it or sold it to another buyer. Currently, the gallery is still intact as is, just waiting for my relaunch.

Furthermore, it turns out that James is also quite wealthy, too. Apparently, while he worked as my personal assistant by day; by night, he was also the secret CEO of a Silicon Valley-based tech company called Verona, which designs and manufactures microchips to sell to various artificial intelligence companies.

Needless to say, my future husband only worked as my personal assistant for the past three years as an excuse to be near to me. Furthermore, according to James, he doesn't want our close working relationship to end, either. Rather, instead of remaining as my personal assistant, he plans on transitioning to become my new agent, determined to help me to promote my career as an artist and a teacher. As well as, of course, serving in the most important role of all: *my husband.*

Currently, it's the first of January, and I'm starting my new year with a hopeful heart. Two months ago, it felt like my world came crashing down, when I lost the election. But now, so much has changed. No longer is my life a soap opera; but instead, it's a romantic comedy. A life that I'm looking forward to live with my one true love.

And now, as I pick up a brand-new canvas from off the floor, I'm ready to start painting a new portrait. And in case you're wondering, the name of this portrait is called…

Happily Ever After…

EPILOGUE

Six Months Later

"Katherine, that's a perfect pose," Martin von Helmsberg smiles, as he eagerly starts chipping away at a block of marble using his chisel.

After marrying James four months ago and honeymooning in Tuscany, I'm back in San Francisco and about ready to launch the reopening of my former art gallery, Bianca & Minola. The opening night is scheduled for two weeks from today. And so, as the starring piece, Martin insisted on sculpting me for the opening night's main exhibit.

Apparently, after glancing at my photograph in the papers, I instantly became his muse. And so, from that horrible press release of *The Scandalous Shrew* article, a new partnership between Martin and I was born.

"You're looking lovely, Mrs. Petruchio," James proudly beams, as he stands right next to Martin.

Even in the studio, he refuses to leave my side. Especially, with me posing in the nude— albeit, I do have a white linen sheet that's currently wrapped around my chest and behind.

"Don't worry, Mr. Petruchio, I'm all covered up," I tease my husband.

Ever since we got married, we've been calling each other Mr. & Mrs. Petruchio more frequently. What can I say? I'm proud to be his wife!

"Keep quiet," Martin hushes us. "I must concentrate."

With my long black hair flowing down my back, I blow a final kiss to my husband and get straight to work by posing as a still life muse. From political nominee to model. Who knew!

In the end, for all of my unique world experiences, according to Martin, the sculpture could only be called none other than…

Katherine, the Great.

SNEAK PREVIEW #1:

Wake Up, Darling

CHAPTER 1

Once Upon a Coma...

With the sun flashing across my face, I struggle to adjust my eyes. But in truth, I can't *open* them, even if I wanted to. But it's not limited to just my eyes. It's also me moving my hands, too. And my legs. And my feet. And my toes. And my arms. And my fingers. It's *everything*. It's my entire body all at once, because I'm *paralyzed*.

Sadly, it took me a long time to come to this conclusion. But lo and behold, I am, indeed, paralyzed. In fact, I'm currently in a deep coma and everyone around me assumes the worst. That I'm lying on death's door. That in a matter of days... *no... hours...* and I'll most likely be declared as dead. Except I'm not. I'm *not* dead. I'm still here!

Strangely enough, I can hear them, but they *can't* hear me. I listen to their loud chatters and gentle whispers. I hear the doctors and the nurses coming in and out, all checking on me periodically. And they've been gossiping about me, too.

Whether I want to or not, I do hear their worries. How tragic my life must have been, according to them. That, for a young woman of thirty years of age, to be in the current vegetative state that I'm in.

To be married to a wealthy senator and yet, for all the money in the world, I still lie unconscious in this bed. Even as a world-famous romance author, I, myself, could never have written such a tragic tale. And yet…

There was an accident. An accident that I can't seem to remember, no matter how much I struggle to recall. Something happened to me and whatever it was, it brought me here. To this very hospital. And now, as I lie in this bed, alone with only my silent thoughts and the sounds of my environment, I'm left wondering one question: why didn't I die?

For some reason, God spared my life. Even with all of the morphine pumping into my body to help me heal, I still can't recall what brought me here… and that alone makes me feel so upset.

No, upset isn't the right word. Instead, I'm *angry*. Better yet, I'm *furious*. I'm furious, because while the world perceives me to be in a coma, I'm still wide awake. Or at least, awake on the inside. Awake and silently listening to my surroundings. Hearing both the good and the bad, all around me.

My main visitors have primarily been the nurses. Mainly females. They cry for me. Many of them were my fans, who previously read all of my romance novels. I can hear their cries, and their well wishes. I know that they all mean well. And truly, I am grateful that my novels have brought them much joy and comfort. That, should I die right here, today; then at least my novels will continue to live on. Some piece of my legacy to pass on into the future. A future absent of any children of my own. *An unfinished life.*

Although I'm aware that I'm indeed, married; but in truth, I can hardly remember my husband. He's like a blackened blur. Both him and his face. But regardless, I do know that he *exists*. I can hear the nurses speak of him, time to time. From what I've gathered, he's a senator. Wealthy, young and handsome.

But has he come to visit me, as of lately? I'm not entirely sure.

However, there's been one man, who's the exception. In fact, he visits me quite often. I can hear him, always weeping. Grieving. His cries of despair might be soft and silent, but I do feel his tear droplets whenever they land upon my face. In truth, it's one of the few exceptions that I can actually *feel* against my entire body. *His endless tears.*

Whenever he enters into my room, the nurses all leave. Often times, he pulls a chair by my bedside and holds my hand. Surprisingly, I can *feel* his touch. It feels warm, nice and safe. But the only problem is that I *can't* move my hand to embrace his, in return. Oh, how I wish that I could! Not being able to touch him, truly feels like hell on earth! It's so unfair and cruel! Oh, how fate cursed me so!

Apart from holding my hand, he doesn't speak much. Honestly, he really doesn't need to. It's not like I can carry a conversation with him, anyways. But either way, he sits there. Silently. Peacefully. Sometimes for only a few short minutes and other times, for several hours on end.

Is he, my husband? I'm not entirely sure. He must be, right? Who else would bother to sit by my constant side, if not for him?

But whomever he is, he does bring me great comfort. Whether he's death or my husband, I don't care. But I do crave his touch. His attention. His affection. I relish on his surprise visits, whenever he comes. And when he's gone, I'm saddened by his absence. Even though I can't speak or touch him, I still *miss* him.

Sometimes, when I'm alone, I often wonder about him. Specifically, of what he looks like. I must have known him in my past. I must have. But then again, my memories are very limited.

Apart from my childhood, career and marital status, everything else is a darkened blur. And if it wasn't for the nurses' gossiping around me, then I'd have never known that I'm married or that my husband is a senator. Sadly, I suppose this accident of mine really did destroy my memories after all…

Again, when my stranger is gone, I genuinely miss him. Even into the late hours of the night, I continue to fantasize about his appearance. Tall or short? Muscular or chubby? Blonde or brunette? Blue eyes or brown? A doctor or a scholar? A businessman or another senator? My husband or someone… *else?*

Mystery, after mystery, after mystery. Whomever my stranger is, I am forever grateful to him. I'm grateful, because apart from the hospital's medical staff, he's the only other person who continues to visit me on a regular basis. He's the only one holding my hand. The only person who encourages me. Motivates me. *Cries for me.*

Again, he doesn't speak much. But there's one phrase that he always utters. Over and over… and over again…

Wake up…

Wake up…

Wake up…

Wake up… *darling…*

His words are spoken like a prayer. He wishes for me to awaken from this coma and to be fair, I do, too. If only to catch a glimpse of his face.

But the truth is, I am awake. *Wide awake.* It's just that my body isn't. My eyes refuse to open, even though I want it to… oh, so desperately! But even when I command it to do so, it still doesn't obey. One way or another, my own body refuses to listen to me… it's like a violent war raging inside of me… and I'm struggling to win this battle…

But apart from my own internal struggles, his voice remains buried in my mind, as my constant motivation. The way he says the word *darling*, it's so touching. It's uttered, using a sweet and tender melody. Like that special word is just for *me*. A private word shared only between him and myself. That my name might be Karly Summers, but to him, I'm his one and only…

DDDDaaarrrllliiinnnggg…

He stretches the vowels and elongates the consonants of this special word, all from the tip of his tongue. He wants me to awaken. So desperately. I can feel it by the sounds of his deep voice. He's trying to enchant me. To encourage me. Anything to have me wake up from this God forsaken coma!

And his words do encourage me. I try. Each day, I try to open my eyes. I practice using every ounce and fiber of my muscles. And one day, I know that I'm going to win this battle. I am going to wake up from this death sentence. I am going to recover. I will overcome my own weakened body, by the sheer power of my mind. I am determined to succeed. I am not a failure, but a fighter. And one day soon, I will open my eyes and rise again!

Because I've decided that this stranger is not death, but my savior. An angel who is desperately trying to keep me here on this earth. To stay alive. To recover. To reunite back with him. To simply *be with him.*

And so, for the next few days, I concentrate. I stay focused. I might still be too weak to wiggle my toes or my fingers, but I know… *I just know…* that I can, at the very least, open my eyes. And if I can open my eyes… then I can finally see him…

And then, on one sunny Sunday, I do. At long last, I finally do open my eyes and once I do, I see a man with bright blonde hair staring back at me and smiling…

SNEAK PREVIEW #2:

The Ambassador's Wife

CHAPTER 1

On a cold December afternoon, Kate stared outside of her grandmother's window to eagerly watch the snow fall upon her family's garden. Precisely one week ago, their garden was covered in bright sunshine, along with blooming white daisies and tall evergreens that flourished throughout their vast open acres. At that time, the crystal blue sky was adorned with pink and emerald green hummingbirds flying high above in the air, all chirping the sweet and joyful melodies of nature. Amazingly, this again, was only but a mere week ago. Come today, all had vanished. The once sunny and cheerful garden was now replaced by a dark and gloomy scene; consisting of a bleak and heavy blanket of thick white snow, accompanied by icy frost and the howling winds of winter.

Unfortunately, due to the stormy weather, Kate and her family were advised to shelter in from the piling snow. Determined to find joy even in the most mundane of circumstances, Kate found enjoyment in gazing outside of her frosty window; all in the hopes of catching a rare glimpse of a fallen snowflake. A snowflake, she thought, was so incredibly beautiful and rare, that only a person patient and willing enough to wait for it, could eventually, see it, one day.

"Kate, come away from that window," cried Shakire, her grandmother. "I need you and Jennifer to help me in the kitchen."

Taking one final glance, Kate hoped for the best. But alas, her hopes were premature; for the winter snow was still progressively falling and there was still no sign of a single snowflake, in near sight.

"We better hurry Kate, I think that she might have a nice surprise for us," said Jennifer, with a twinkle in her eye.

Jennifer was Kate's sister--her twin sister to be precise. Both sisters were identical twins, with the same facial structures, blue eyes, fair complexions, petite body structures and tall in height. However, the only exception between them were their hair colorings, in which Jennifer's hair was naturally blonde, while Kate's was brown. Other than this singular difference, both girls were identical; even down to the very same freckle located right underneath their chins.

However, it wasn't very difficult to distinguish the twin sisters apart; for once they spoke, it became abundantly clear, as to which sister was whom. Jennifer, the lively, romantic and passionate twin, often spoke carefree to whatever and whichever came directly to her mind; whereas, Kate, the practical, shy and reserved twin, analyzed her thoughts and calculated her words more carefully before sharing them publicly with others. While Kate preferred to spend her Saturday nights at home reading a Jane Austen book, along with a warm cup of Earl of Grey tea; Jennifer, in contrast, was more interested on attending parties and finding her modern-day Prince Charming. Due to their opposing natures, Shakire often referred to them as the sun and the moon; in which Jennifer, along with her bright yellow hair, was the sun and Kate, with her shiny and dark hair, the moon. Ironically, this reference was entirely appropriate for them too, since their own given middle names meant exactly that in the Turkish language. Just like the sun, Jennifer was named Jennifer Guneş; and just like the moon, Kate was named Kate Aylin.

At seventeen years old, the twin sisters came to visit Shakire's home for their winter holidays. Located on the northwestern coast of Türkiye, bordering the Marmara and Aegean Seas, Shakire lived in a small but modest city called Balikesir. Their mother, a native of the land, had married their father, an American soldier, who was previously stationed there in their small town. As a result, the twin sisters were born and raised in New York City. While they primarily resided in New York for their schooling, their winter and summer breaks were spent almost entirely and exclusively in Türkiye with Shakire.

Following their grandmother's directions, the twin sisters walked into their kitchen and saw Shakire already seated at the table. To their surprise, right next to their grandmother, were three separate small cups of coffee. Without their prior knowledge, the warm beverage had already been carefully brewed and poured right into the golden ceramic expresso cups, along with their matching saucers.

"I thought that you needed help?" asked Kate, surprised by the sight before her eyes.

"Actually, I still do," admitted Shakire, with a huge and bright smile, as she took her first sip of coffee. "Although I might have already taken the liberty to prepare us some nice Turkish coffee; now, I'm in need of your help to drink them."

"Wonderful!" exclaimed Jennifer, happily. "Does this mean, what I think it means?"

"Yes, it does," replied Shakire. "Once we finish drinking our coffee, we'll do a little round of fortune telling with the coffee grounds. A nice unexpected treat to a cold and dreary winter's afternoon, don't you think?"

Excitingly, both sisters were happily in agreement. Drinking Turkish coffee was one of their most favorite pastimes at Shakire's home. Coffee time was also their bonding time together. In addition to fortune telling, Shakire also used this opportunity to share tall tales and exotic stories about their history and culture with them; and in return, the sisters also confided about their own secret dreams and life pursuits to their grandmother. Even though their coffee readings were entirely for fun, it was also often claimed by several other family members and nearby neighbors, that Shakire's predictions did actually come true, from time to time. Although Shakire tried her best to teach and share this natural gift to her granddaughters, the art of coffee reading, or tasseography, was something that just came naturally to oneself and wasn't a trait that could really be learned, nor taught. Therefore, rather than attempting to decipher the meaning for themselves, the twin sisters simply quietly sat back and enjoyed themselves, as they listened to Shakire's reading, instead.

"There, I'm done!" shouted Jennifer, as she quickly gulped her last sip of coffee, and then, hastily flipped the empty cup upside down and back onto her saucer. Upon closing the cup, Jennifer promptly spun the object around her in a circle, and then at long last, she made a wish.

"That was fast," observed Kate; who, in contrast, preferred to savor each and every last bit and morsel of her coffee.

"Alright, my dear Jennifer. Let's have a look at it," Shakire instructed.

Following her grandmother's instructions, Jennifer quickly handed her cup and saucer over to Shakire. Upon receiving it, Shakire proceeded to flip the cup right side up; after which, she slowly began to inspect the dried coffee grounds.

"Hmm," began Shakire. "I see several lines in your cup. My dear, I believe that you shall travel the world."

Happy with her grandmother's prediction, Jennifer privately smiled to herself. Unbeknownst to most, Jennifer had secretly dreamed of traveling the world.

"I also see a large diamond ring, with lots of coins," Shakire continued, "You will marry wealthy and also be a very famous woman, at the same time."

Bringing Jennifer's cup even closer towards her, Shakire slowly pulled down her eyeglasses to carefully examine the remaining coffee grounds directly with her naked eye. After a few extra silent minutes of concentration, Shakire finally spoke and said "But…"

"But? Is something wrong?" asked Jennifer, suddenly concerned with the possibility of something being potentially troubling and an exception to perfection.

"Nothing to worry about, my dear," replied Shakire, as she attempted to console her granddaughter. "But," she continued, "I do see two rings. I'm afraid that you will marry twice, after all."

"Twice?" asked Kate, this time, who was equally surprised by this particular revelation.

"Yes, two marriages," Shakire confirmed. "Although you'll marry your first husband at a young age, your second marriage will occur much later on. Unlike your first, your second marriage will be a happier, prosperous and longer union, with wealth and children. He will also be a far better and more ideal match for you, too."

"I suppose that as long as my second husband is far wealthier than the first, then I'm perfectly fine and content with that," laughed Jennifer, not at all bothered by the prospect of marrying twice.

"Either way, I shall record this information into my diary, and in twenty years' time, we'll know as to whether or not you were right," added Jennifer, boldly.

"Jennifer, must you write and record about everything inside of your diary? Our coffee times are meant to be for fun only!" exclaimed Kate.

"Kate, if I'm to become a famous celebrity one day, then I might as well start recording this information now, in time for my future biography. But enough about me, it's time to look at Kate's now," said Jennifer, as she was now determined to shift the focus away from herself and onto her sister.

"Alright my dear Kate, please finish up your cup, and then, let's go ahead and take a look," Shakire instructed.

Under any normal of circumstances, Kate would have much better preferred to have taken her sweet time to savor each and every last sip of her coffee, while eating either a sweet pastry or a chocolate bar on the side. For Kate, preparing, serving and drinking Turkish coffee was an art, in which there was a famous Turkish proverb: a cup of coffee amongst strangers can spark a new lifetime of friendship. And indeed, Kate was a true believer of this very wise, yet true proverb.

Following her grandmother's request, Kate drank the remainder of her coffee. Unlike Jennifer's coffee, which was bubbly and sweet with sugar; Kate drank her coffee plain, strong, dark and bitter. In contrast to Jennifer's sugary coffee style, Kate's coffee's aroma was bold and masculine, and the color of her drink was as dark as charcoal. To top it all off, the rim of her cup was covered by a thick layer of foam; similar to the same sea foam found throughout the Mediterranean Sea.

After taking her final sip, Kate turned her cup upside down onto the saucer to allow her coffee grounds to fall and settle along its surface. Since the shapes and symbols formed by the coffee grounds were meant serve as a helpful guide to her grandmother's fortune telling, Kate took extra care to give a good and thorough spin around. After a few brief moments to allow the coffee grounds to dry, Kate slowly handed her coffee cup and saucer over to her grandmother.

"Thank you, my dear," said Shakire, as she graciously took the cup and saucer from Kate's hands.

While Shakire focused on the coffee cup, Kate sat nervously awaiting her grandmother's predictions. Although Shakire had previously read her coffee grounds a hundred times over; most of the times they were rushed, light-hearted and purely for fun, without much thought or effort. However, today, Shakire appeared to be in a more serious mood. Unlike before, she seemed to be in full concentration and so, Kate wondered if this time, her predictions today were meant to come true.

Lifting the cup up from its saucer, Shakire stared deep into the pits of her coffee grounds. Carefully, she examined each image and symbol with extra care, as she traced each image with her index finger. For a long while, Shakire remained silent, in full concentration. As the clock ticked away, Kate began to wonder and worry as to what was taking her grandmother so long to reveal her predictions.

"Grandmother, are you not finding anything in my cup?" asked Kate, finally, breaking their silence.

"No, I definitely do see something; but Kate, you have a very interesting cup," revealed Shakire, at long last.

"I do see books, a large university, podium, and an audience…you will be a teacher, one day, Kate," Shakire predicted.

"Well, that's to be expected," huffed Jennifer, sarcastically. "We all know as to just how much Kate loves her books and school. But what about marriage?"

Apparently, Jennifer was far more eager to inquire about Kate's future, than Kate was to ask about herself.

"I do see marriage, too," replied Shakire. "But Kate's marriage will come about under very peculiar circumstances; but I dare say, in the end, hers will be a tremendously happy and romantic marriage, indeed."

"Peculiar, in which way?" asked Kate, most curiously.

"Yes, peculiar, in which way?" echoed Jennifer.

"I cannot say for certain," answered Shakire. "But Kate, circumstances beyond your control will bring you to him. Fate, it seems, will cross your paths together, in the most unexpected way. Furthermore, you'll know that it's him, when he first kisses you…in the snow."

"The snow?" exclaimed both Kate and Jennifer, excited by that revelation.

"Yes, the snow," Shakire confirmed. "And Kate, I do see a little snowflake in your cup, too."

"A snowflake?" asked Kate, stunned by this new prediction. How amazing that only but a few minutes ago, Kate sat ever-so patiently staring away at her window, and waiting and hoping to see a snowflake. How strange that her one wish would somehow magically appear inside of her cup?

"Yes," replied Shakire. "There's a snowflake and a very beautiful one at that, I dare say. The edges are rough, but the design is almost as beautiful as a winter rose. And right next to the snowflake, is a lovely white pearl."

"Oh, that's Kate's favorite gem, the pearl," interrupted Jennifer.

"Yes, I know. And next to the snowflake and pearl, is the man," added Shakire.

"Kate is going to marry a snowman," Jennifer playfully teased.

"No, that isn't it," replied Shakire. "Kate, one day, this man is going to fall madly in love you. But first, you have to overcome some obstacles. Like all important tasks, you'll have to climb your mountain, before you acquire your treasure. But in the end, it will be all worth it; for he's your soul mate."

"How romantic!" cried Jennifer. "A kiss in the snow, snowflakes, roses, pearls and all! It must be true love, Kate!"

Kate blushed. Only time would tell.

ABOUT THE AUTHOR

Kristina Stangl is an American author. She was born and raised in San Francisco, California, USA. She holds a Master's degree in Public Administration, MPA; a Bachelor of Arts in International Relations, with a minor in Middle East and Islamic Studies from San Francisco State University; along with Teaching English as a Foreign Language (TEFL) credentials from the University of Toronto, Ontario Institute for Studies in Education. Before writing her first novel, Kristina previously worked in both the public and private sectors, having served in the United States federal government for nine years. In addition to writing, Kristina enjoys traveling across the globe and visiting famous and historical sites, which she documents on her social media accounts. To date, she has traveled to over thirteen countries, three continents, and speaks three languages. When Kristina is not traveling or writing, she's at home experimenting with baking new desserts, pies and other sweet treats.